ICE

ROYAL BASTARDS MC—ELKO, NEVADA
BOOK ONE

SCARLETT BLACK

Ice
Copyright © 2020 By Scarlett Black

Acknowledgments
Cover Art: Jay Aheer
Cover Image: Lindee Robinson
Content/Developmental Editing: Rogue Readers
Editing: Rebecca Ernst Vazquez

To Author M. Merin, from the bottom of my heart, a great big thank you. I am so blessed to have met such a great friend in you. I am so happy to be included in this series and that you thought of me. This opportunity is everything.

Special thanks to Rebecca Vazquez, girl, I am so happy that we found each other. I have enjoyed working with and growing together. Thank you, for all your help from the big things to the small ones. You rock.

Melissa Rivera, you are my rock and kept me going. Everyday you give me support. You do so much more than edit. Don't worry, I am working on not freaking out. And sprinkling it out like glitter throughout the day. :)

To the Bitches Without Borders, I made it this far because of you, with every book you buy and read. Dreams do come true. Thank you.

ROYAL BASTARDS CODE

PROTECT: The club and your brothers come before anything else, and must be protected at all costs. **CLUB** is **FAMILY**.

RESPECT: Earn it & Give it. Respect club law. Respect the patch. Respect your brothers. Disrespect a member and there will be hell to pay.

HONOR: Being patched in is an honor, not a right. Your colors are sacred, not to be left alone, and **NEVER** let them touch the ground.

OL' LADIES: Never disrespect a member's or brother's Ol' Lady. **PERIOD.**

CHURCH is **MANDATORY.**

LOYALTY: Takes precedence over all, including well-being.

HONESTY: Never **LIE, CHEAT,** or **STEAL** from another member or the club.

TERRITORY: You are to respect your brother's property and follow their Chapter's club rules.

TRUST: Years to earn it…seconds to lose it.

NEVER RIDE OFF: Brothers do not abandon their family.

They say I am cold as ice.

You could say that's how I got my road name or the fact that no one can get through my thick ruthless exterior.

I've done gruesome things that even the devil would be disgusted by. The demons that reside within demand that I release them no matter the cost.

I don't know what it's like to love. I don't believe that it actually exists. Life ain't no damn fairytale.

I've seen beautiful women, and I've been with lots of them.

But it's the pain in her eyes that I crave to consume.

I want it all, her flesh, heart, and soul. I may lose everything to keep her.

But even the fires of hell couldn't keep me away. I would battle even my Brothers just to protect her.

She's mine for better or for worse.

ICE

ICE

PROLOGUE

Two years ago...

All the Battle Born Presidents sit around the table at the Las Vegas clubhouse. Stryker, the Mother Chapter President, sits at the head of the table, followed by the Reno Prez, Blade, Fuego, the Sacramento Prez, and me, Ice, the President of the Elko Chapter of the Battle Born MC.

"Rancid agreed to patch over the Elko clubhouse to the Royal Bastards MC," Stryker informs us. It's a decision we all hesitated to make. One that I want to avoid but know that it is here nonetheless. We share the profits and it allows us ties into their resources. Being sister chapters, they will also exchange property for us to expand Battle Born into their territory. The biggest reason is the ATF agents hidden in plain sight looking for the Cartel King we buried in the desert. Since the war between the Cartel and the Battle Born MC got hot, they've been on our ass. This shift will get the scent off our brothers, and deliver retribution quietly to those who deserve it.

I hated to leave Battle Born behind, but on the other

hand, the Royal Bastards have been in my blood for a long time. Drawing way back into my youth, it was circumstances that brought me to the Battle Born clubhouse first, but it seems the past has come a-calling and is dragging me back to my roots. Time for the devil to collect his dues. Battle Born has had bad blood with the cartel over the years, so this change is making for stronger security for us at the border. It's a game of chess, and if it stops the bloodshed, I will do it to keep men alive and out of prison. It is what needs to happen. Alliances will strengthen our borders and weaken our enemies.

It was a strategic move to join the MCs together, making our national ties even stronger. As long as I have my cut and my brothers at my back, I will wear it proudly.

They all look at me for our chapter's vote, there is no going back. "We voted Aye."

The Elko clubhouse is now property of the Royal Bastards MC.

ONE

Ice

They say I'm a fucking bastard. I'm not. There are reasons I am the way I am. Cold hard fucking truths about life have made the dick most see me as. Fuck them and fuck you if you believe them. You probably should though, I will take your life for any reason that I see fit. I am the Prez of the Royal Bastards MC, Elko chapter.

It's time to get lost in the haze of the hours that swirl by. Blowing out the long drag of bud from my lungs, I smirk at Tina, the blonde-haired biker bitch who rides my dick at my will. Her hair swings wide to the right. She is as broken as me. It is what makes us work. Tina is a showcase of dark desires, wearing nothing from head to toe.

My fingers tangle into the silky strands of her hair. Tina bites her lip and pulls her body to mine, straddling my lap. Nothing is left to the imagination with her pink pussy on full display for me. I lick up her neck in one long line to her chin. She breathes out a moan of satisfaction. She grinds her pussy over my jeans while her hands push my cut as far back as possible. No bitch is allowed to touch the cut. "You know the rules," I snarl at the cunt. Gone is her chance to have the happy ending I'm getting.

Abruptly, I stand and carry her over to the pool table, dropping her on her ass as a ball is hit and skids past, barely missing her. The balls scatter around her body and she becomes part of the game. I pull my zipper down just enough to get my dick out. If she is hurt and stops me from getting what I want, I'll drop the motherfucker stupid enough to take that shot.

Pulling a condom out of my pants, I rip it open with my teeth before sheathing my steel cock. My nails dig into her thighs, pulling Tina to me. Her hands are behind her back, making her arch her pierced tits toward me.

In one thrust, I bury myself in her balls deep. I take everything from her body. Every piece becomes mine. I feed off her excitement, the lust that oozes from her pores. Biting down on her nipple, I gradually ease away, dragging my teeth along her flesh until I meet metal, my tongue swirling around the bud. She groans and rocks her hips, wanting more and expecting it. With a quick bite, I release the pain and rain down all I can, pounding into her body with mine. It's not enough. I crave more. I need to see the flash of pain in her eyes. Instead of holding onto her, I grip the edge of the pool table.

The ball cracks and drops into a pocket in the background, but I am too far gone. I need the release, the view of something else, a reprieve from the ugliness inside. The demons chase me. Endless faces of the dead. Men I have killed. Brothers I have buried. All their faces never-ending and always with me. I hammer my cock into her with a force that would make most women cry. She holds herself up, because if she doesn't, we'll never fuck again. Tina winces when I bring my weight down onto her with my next thrust. Her eyes dilate and the adrenaline to survive floods her bloodstream. I want it. If I could drink it from her body, I would.

The last shot is taken and the ball comes barreling from the opposite end of the pool table toward her hand. My hand darts out and I take her by her neck. Choking her with my grip, I pull her toward me just in time. Tina chokes on air, gasping for life. My dick twitches before I come. I don't let go of her neck for as long as I can before it is too much for her. Her hand, at least, was saved from a broken finger.

My hold loosens and her lungs fight for air, inflating as fast as she can gather life back into them. A tear leaks out of the corner of her eye. I can't stop myself from taking it into my mouth with a swipe of my tongue. Tina holds on tight, not only to me but to the life she just seen flash before her eyes.

Pulling out, I tuck myself away and zip up. Leaving her where she's at, I stomp around the table to the stupid fuck who almost hurt her. Chains knows what's coming and braces himself for my fist that flies for his face. If you have punched a person before, you know it hurts. Every bone in my hand protests with the blow I deliver to his cheekbone. His head snaps back, but he stays on his feet.

Had he fallen, Chains would find out what my boot tastes like. Done for the night, I head off to my room frustrated. The same shit, just a different day. Something needs to change and soon, before killing becomes a pastime to break up the boredom. Over thirty years, I've chased ass, drugs, and cash. It's been a train wreck of chaos, losing its luster after all these years. I still have a lot of life left. It's time for something new—I just don't know what that is yet.

TWO

Ice

My head pounds from the whiskey and drugs. Cottonmouth is a side effect from all that I did the night before. Hitting fifty-five this year, my body is telling me to slow the fuck down, but I can't ever. Rest is for the dead. After I wash my face and brush my teeth, I dress in my workout clothes, a loose tank and shorts.

Stretching out in my room, I chug a full bottle of water before I hit the trail out back behind the clubhouse, a tough terrain through the mountain. My lungs burn and protest with the incline. The workout is a bruising punishment after the night I had. My feet pound into the dirt, kicking up dust. After three miles, my blood pressure picks up and I am in the zone to chase the last three. I push myself all the way back to the clubhouse before I lift weights. Today is arm day and I stack the weights on the bench.

I'm almost done when my VP, River, walks in with his phone in his hand. "Prez, Blade needs to speak with you."

Sitting up from the bench, I whip my shirt off to dry my hands and face before taking the phone from him. "Ice."

"Hey," Blade starts. "The coyote is in Las Vegas. Harley is supposed to be down there for some gig she got. Can you take her?" The coyote is code for the investor on stateside who has been helping the Cartel with funds and connections. He has been hard to trace.

"Did I just fucking hear you ask me, the Prez, to babysit an Ol' Lady?" I'm fucking with Blade. Harley's Ol' Man was the VP of the Battle Born Las Vegas chapter. Mad Max had an accident and died a few years back. She's a good woman. This is about business, but if we are being listened to, we make the call as casual as possible while getting the information across.

"Quit fucking around. I know you'll be here by sundown." ATF has been snooping around them, and let's just say I've been cleaning up. That way, Battle Born has been appearing clean while we tie up loose ends. Plus, it's been a good trade-off, keeping our clubs flush with cash.

"Or what? You'll tell your fuckin' dad on me? Is he heading up for your new little brat to be born?" I poke at him a little for kicks. Blade's the son of Stryker, the Prez of the Battle Born Mother Chapter.

"Nah, I'll kick your ass myself. Stryker and most of the Battle Born will be here." Meaning a hit on the man won't blow back on them.

Blade's cocky response causes a deep chuckle to erupt from my chest. "Be there soon." Passing the phone back to River, I ask, "You got the clubhouse while I'm gone?"

"Aye, brother. Stay out of trouble." River claps my back and heads out. Since I've got a long ride across the state of Nevada, I decide to take a shower and slam an energy drink before I hit the road to Reno.

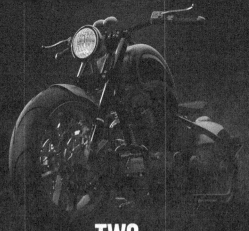

TWO

Ice

My head pounds from the whiskey and drugs. Cottonmouth is a side effect from all that I did the night before. Hitting fifty-five this year, my body is telling me to slow the fuck down, but I can't ever. Rest is for the dead. After I wash my face and brush my teeth, I dress in my workout clothes, a loose tank and shorts.

Stretching out in my room, I chug a full bottle of water before I hit the trail out back behind the clubhouse, a tough terrain through the mountain. My lungs burn and protest with the incline. The workout is a bruising punishment after the night I had. My feet pound into the dirt, kicking up dust. After three miles, my blood pressure picks up and I am in the zone to chase the last three. I push myself all the way back to the clubhouse before I lift weights. Today is arm day and I stack the weights on the bench.

I'm almost done when my VP, River, walks in with his phone in his hand. "Prez, Blade needs to speak with you."

Sitting up from the bench, I whip my shirt off to dry my hands and face before taking the phone from him. "Ice."

"Hey," Blade starts. "The coyote is in Las Vegas. Harley is supposed to be down there for some gig she got. Can you take her?" The coyote is code for the investor on stateside who has been helping the Cartel with funds and connections. He has been hard to trace.

"Did I just fucking hear you ask me, the Prez, to babysit an Ol' Lady?" I'm fucking with Blade. Harley's Ol' Man was the VP of the Battle Born Las Vegas chapter. Mad Max had an accident and died a few years back. She's a good woman. This is about business, but if we are being listened to, we make the call as casual as possible while getting the information across.

"Quit fucking around. I know you'll be here by sundown." ATF has been snooping around them, and let's just say I've been cleaning up. That way, Battle Born has been appearing clean while we tie up loose ends. Plus, it's been a good trade-off, keeping our clubs flush with cash.

"Or what? You'll tell your fuckin' dad on me? Is he heading up for your new little brat to be born?" I poke at him a little for kicks. Blade's the son of Stryker, the Prez of the Battle Born Mother Chapter.

"Nah, I'll kick your ass myself. Stryker and most of the Battle Born will be here." Meaning a hit on the man won't blow back on them.

Blade's cocky response causes a deep chuckle to erupt from my chest. "Be there soon." Passing the phone back to River, I ask, "You got the clubhouse while I'm gone?"

"Aye, brother. Stay out of trouble." River claps my back and heads out. Since I've got a long ride across the state of Nevada, I decide to take a shower and slam an energy drink before I hit the road to Reno.

THREE

Harley

"I still can't believe they want me for the cover of the magazine. It's been years since I've modeled." I complain a bit, frustrated and self-conscious of my body. Vegas, Blade's wife, drops a spoon into her bowl and Dana gazes at me with a confused look on her face.

"You're crazy," Dana informs me. She is married to my son, Axl. "You may not have the crazy super lean super-model body from twenty years ago, but you're hot as hell!"

"I still can't believe I agreed. When my old manager reached out to me, she was more excited than me." I was too shocked to comprehend the words and what they meant. It also struck a chord inside. I modeled at a time when the world was perfect. I had it all, a future still with Maddox. I met him at a bike shoot in downtown Las Vegas. It was a live shoot and the steamy gaze from him captured me in an instant. I can remember the details like it was just yesterday.

"Turn a little to your left and look over your shoulder," the

camera man instructs. The fan picks up my long blonde hair and wisps it around my face.

A lean muscular biker stands with his arms crossed over his chest. His eyes are glued to my exposed flesh and the tiny red string bikini. My heart beats in my chest in response to his piercing stare. The flex of his biceps when he notices my attention is solely on him in the crowd of men around him causes me to gasp.

"That's it, more of that," the camera man interrupts us momentarily. Something in his cocky smile calls to me and dares me to show off more. Biting my lip, I tease him back and take on the dare. I pose in ways that would make the cover on a different kind of magazine, not for motorcycles.

The erotic display causes the crowd to thicken and the excitement from the catcalls and whistles changes the environment to electrifying. I work every part of my body over the display bike for sale. It was to be auctioned off on-stage after the shoot. My manager bounces from foot-to-foot, knowing this is a huge moment for me.

Once the pictures are captured and the emcee comes on, the stage darkens, casting a spotlight on me to model the bike for the sale. Behind us, the screen lights up and the photos of me flash on the backdrop. It's all a haze because all I can see is the man who has dared me to take it all, leaving nothing here. My body is draped and grinding on the bike he intends on buying.

"Twenty thousand dollars," he hollers. "I'll pay more, because…she…belongs to me."

Most would think he was talking about the bike my hands are gripping to hold me up, but the biker's intent is me. The fluttering in my chest is unbearable. The anticipation of this

ICE

flirty game we started has a cost and what will that be? Not that I could stop myself even if I want to.

"Sold," the emcee declares.

The biker should head into the office and write out a check for his bid, but he doesn't. He places both hands at the edge of the stage and jumps up. With every step, he commands attention and purpose. His cocky smile is in full force. In return, my lips pick up and I smile back, my cheeks feeling the strain. His swagger is intoxicating.

What I didn't expect was what came next. I thought he would claim his new motorcycle. He claimed me. Large, strong, calloused hands graze my waist and protectively hold me to him. Into my ear, he whispers, "I'd give everything I own to do that all over again."

My fingers hold on to this hulky sweet man when his lips take mine. His patch says, 'Mad Max' and he is as crazy as they get.

I push aside the pain, not wanting to relive the despair that festers inside like a cancer that will never leave my body. The day Maddox died from a tragic accident, a piece of me went with him. When I look at Axl, our son, he is him. Except his eyes, which are green like mine. But his hair and features are all his father's. My heart burns with regret. Time was stolen along with my happiness. If it weren't for Axl and his family, I would be a leaf blowing in the wind.

Dana holds onto my hand. "I know it was special, the day you two met. Do this for you. Go down there and show off that smoking body all of us are jealous of. He would absolutely love to see you do this. Kill it, for all of us."

11

I'm not as fragile as I was before. There is no way, even a year ago, that I could have done this. I'm not chasing a ghost, because I want to move forward. I want to find a way to say goodbye, not forever but enough to move on. I crave freedom from these chains more than anything. I just need to go, even with the fear of standing in a bikini again for a throwback cover edition. I need to find me, and I'm ready.

Lifting the corner of my mouth, I cave. "Alright, but you know what this means."

"No," Vegas smarts, "I am not drinking any of your green smoothie stuff or running with you. Woman, you are some kind of superwoman. I cannot do it. I will support you from a distance."

"Vegas, I meant shopping." I chuckle. "I can't go to Las Vegas without some flashy, trendy, sexy clothes."

"Thank God!"

"That, we will help with," Dana confirms.

"Nice to know where my limits are with you two. Thanks."

Dana taps her chin. "You know, you could just borrow my clothes. I have tons of heels, leather pants, halter tops. Stuff I don't use since we had Maddie. The girls and I don't go clubbing anymore."

Over the next hour, I find five outfits from Dana's closet that I can wear for every occasion while I'm there. It was fun to model for the girls and test out my skills that were hidden deep from my youth. The whole time I spent with them washed away any doubts I had about going. Their lives are so full, and they have ambition to find and explore life. I cannot wilt away and watch life pass me by. I am determined to live my best life and what better way to kick it off than in Sin City?

FOUR

Ice

It's strange pulling up to the Reno clubhouse all alone. Never have I not been with the brothers of either the Battle Born or the Royal Bastards MC on the road. This trip, however, requires a solo ride. My life revolves around the club, they are my family. I could've had one, but it wasn't in the cards for this old dog.

We were young and she was in love. I tried to settle down and be the man I thought I needed to be. Problem was, she hated the club and the roar of the bike. She wanted kids and thought I would grow out of the lifestyle. The longer we were together, I realized we would never work. I wanted the wild life and she wanted a reliable man. I wanted hot, passionate nights and no kids. We didn't last long after that. My early twenties feel like a lifetime ago, and that was the last girlfriend I had.

My boot swings forward once the bike comes to a halt and I jam the kickstand down before I turn off the motor. I flew down the freeway with nothing but the wind, sun, my thoughts, and good music to keep me company. It was good to get away from the usual shit for a bit. As soon as I stand, pain shoots up my spine as I stretch and curse, twisting from side to side.

"It gets harder, the older you get, on the long runs like that. At least that's what my old man tells me," Blade, the cocky bastard, smarts off to me.

"I ain't fucking dead yet. I'll ride till I die. You ain't shit." I swing an arm around Blade's back. I've known this asshole since he was in diapers. Time has flown by like the miles in my life, decades of history, and I couldn't be prouder of the man who is the Prez of his MC. "What's this bullshit you have me here for?" I have a job to do, but the thought of the events Harley has planned makes me want to turn around and head home.

"Axl has Dana and their kid. Vegas is about to deliver our little girl. Everyone is coming up here who can, and half the MC in Sacramento is heading over the hill for this too. Crazy, brother. If you would have told me I would be tied to a princess of the MC and all this, I would have said you were fucking crazy. I'm happy though."

"So, you're saying I'm the only man who doesn't have ties to this birthing shit. Alright, I'm in for a trip to Las Vegas." Ideas start to formulate in my mind. A weekend in Sin City? "Sign me up, brother."

Axl pops his head out from the garage. "You aren't going down there to fuck around. You'll have my mom." He doesn't know about the hits on the ATF informant. Only a handful does. I trust all my brothers, from both clubs, but this information is only within a small circle.

"And? Your point being what?" I cock a brow at the momma's boy. "Maybe she's due for some fun." I was gonna say dick, but I respect the Ol' Ladies, especially Harley. She's one classy bitch.

"Fun, yeah, but she isn't in that headspace, and I'll remind you, she's a grandmother."

A deep chuckle then a boisterous laugh echoes out of the garage. Tank's big ass head pops out. "Take my woman to and from that beautiful place in one piece. We need her back home safely."

"What the fuck?" I'm about to ask Tank why the hell he said that when I know he has a lady, but he and Axl start to wrestle around for a minute when it dawns on me—Tank must have had a boner for his friend's mom since puberty. Who the hell wouldn't?

Tank pushes Axl back and they calm down and join us. Axl adjusts his shirt and nods to my bike. "You do realize that you can't take her on that, right?" When I don't say anything, it's clear I planned on her jumping on with me.

Tank's grin stretches across his face. "Oh, this just got interesting. You know she has two little dogs that go everywhere with her too, right?" Once again, I don't respond. How the hell would I know this?

"You can borrow the SUV from the MC. There will be enough room for all of you in there. Mom doesn't leave the dogs behind. They go with her everywhere."

"I don't remember her having fuckin' little dogs. When did this happen?"

"A few years ago." Axl glares and the conversation is shut down. How can I say no? That means she got them after her Ol' Man passed. "That's right, they all go. Be at the house by seven. We'll load the SUV tonight and you all can leave early tomorrow."

I turn to get on the bike and haul ass out of there when Blade grips my shoulder. "C'mon. We got some food and beer inside. Hot shower and whatever else you need." I can't explain what it is that holds me there. I could run to Las Vegas alone and get this little mess taken care of. Except the target is one of the investors who is also sponsoring Harley's event. Very suspicious of the asshole that they are sending me in to watch over her. I never do shit for women or what other members do for favors, but I don't have a choice today. The reaper called and I answered.

"Mom!" Axl bangs with a tight fist loudly on her front door. "Fucking hell. I told her to be ready." He fumbles for the keys in his pockets when the front door opens. Last night, I didn't get to see her. She was out while we loaded her bags. The woman who stands before me doesn't look like she's aged in twenty damn years. Her long legs could bring a man home every night. I'm going to have a stiff dick if she's wearing those shorts all the way there.

"Axl, don't," she reprimands, steps out, and jabs another bag in his direction. Her arms swing around me and she gives me a big hug. "Ice, how long has it been? Two years?" She grabs onto my shoulders and holds me there. "You look the same. Still handsome as the devil himself." She winks and steps back as two small dogs start to bark and bite at my jeans. Harley scolds them before picking them up. "Meet Bella and Ben. Axl bought them for me."

Axl helpfully moves her along and asks, "You ready? Have your phone charged and cash?"

16

Ignoring his comment, she shakes her head, waltzing away over to the vehicle, setting the dogs on the backseat. "Bye, honey." She waves and jumps into the front seat with the small bag slung around her back.

Axl turns to me and the look in his eyes says it all. I was called to take care of the most important person in his life, his mom. "We'll be good. I got this." Hitting his shoulder, I get in the vehicle and clear my throat. "Seatbelt, Harley."

"You're shitting me, right?" Harley pokes at me, waiting for a response.

"Nope. I have strict orders to take you there and back unharmed."

She grins before pulling the seatbelt over her lap. The bastard in me sneaks a glance at her exposed soft skin. All this time, she was right there and never have I had so much as a thought of her as more, except the last couple of years. It was one day not that long ago, her eyes showed me a different woman. She wasn't the same and never would be, but that woman called to me. The torment warped her mind. Gone was the fairytale life she had. In its place was the sting of death. I've long past outgrown the questions of why things happen to us. It doesn't happen to us, it just happens. I live my life waiting and watching. I situate myself to sit where I want when it does go down. Maddox was my brother, but temptation is waving a red flag in my face. I remind myself of that and snap my attention forward. I may want to test my limits with Harley, but it would also test my brotherhood.

17

Harley

I don't know what I ever did to Ice. He's hardly said two words to me in hours. Is he upset that he had to come? I didn't want to make anyone be here with me. Instead of thinking too much into it, I pull out my Kindle and settle into a book about an arranged mafia marriage.

Miles pass by and I'm lost in the words before I realize we have stopped at a gas station. "Would you like for me to get you something?" I ask, hoping to break the awkwardness between us.

"No." Ice gets out and ignores me, slamming his door shut.

"Okay. I'll let the dogs out, then run inside," I grumble to myself, opening the door.

"You can't go that far alone at a truck stop, Harley. Wait and I will go," he bites back.

Setting my hands on my hips, I stare over the hood at him until he turns around to face me. "Who's here, Ice?" I wave my hands around an empty parking lot. "We are in the middle of the desert." Exasperated with his coldness, I turn to open the door when a hand slams down in front of me.

"Just because you can't see the threat doesn't mean something is not there." He grits out each word.

Tiny tingles flash up my spine and a fire long gone ignites ever so lightly. For a long time, I haven't had a reason to get upset. My family walked on eggshells to keep my life easy. In a way, it's a relief that I don't have to pretend to have my feelings and actions in poised control. I'm tired of the bullshit and I won't spend another minute with the asshole. "I know that." Biting back feels great, and now that I opened it, I can't stop. "I don't like that you don't want to be here. I'm sorry they made you come. Just take me back." I don't want it bad enough to fight the whole way there and back.

"Harley," Ice stalls, his hand lowering the nozzle to the gas pump, setting it back on the hook. With bated breath, I watch as he rounds the car and stops just in front of me. He gently takes my hand and the air is stolen from my lungs. His touch is soft and sweet, but his eyes are firm and his voice is commanding. "I'm a hard man. I don't do the soft shit you are used to. Life has shaped me into who I am. Ignore the bastard with bad manners. I know you are used to better."

Ice has incredibly beautiful gray-blue eyes with wrinkles at the corners, a strong jawline peppered with brown and gray hair, and his skin is tan but weathered from the sun. He's not soft, and even now when he tries, he's direct while trying for tenderness.

"Okay" is the only word I can manage to allow to escape. For the first time, I see a man. One who makes me think of possibilities. Those ideas are scary because they have not been alive in years.

He nods once, then lets my hand go and steps back. "Let me pump the gas and I'll walk with you. We stay together," Ice amends in a more agreeable tone.

"Yes, sir," I joke and cross my arms, lean up against the side of the car, and watch his muscles flex in his back. The muscles in his arms ripple from the simple action of pumping gas. When the nozzle is put away, I open the door and the dogs excitedly jump out. Together, we walk over to the rest area. From the corner of my eye, I watch him watch me. Unspoken words and the silence speak volumes. I suspect he's a man of little words and a lot of action. My skin tingles picturing him in action.

Ice doesn't seem to be in a hurry and allows the dogs a few minutes to burn off some steam running around. "I'm surprised you were okay with me bringing them." I point out, "Axl said I could leave the dogs with him, but he thought I might miss them since I was going to be gone for so long." I'm not sure what I was expecting, but Ice is in a whole other category of man. Seeing how he is firsthand, it makes me relieved that Axl insisted I bring them to keep me company. I always had a buffer around the brothers and never really spent one-on-one time with them.

"I wasn't asked. Preferably, no, I don't think you should have brought them. They could be a problem." Gone is the nice guy who tried to mend fences. His shitty attitude is pissing me off. Ice will ruin my whole trip if he keeps this up. Why the hell couldn't they send someone else?

"And now that's my problem, when you could have mentioned that before we left?" I don't wait, and even if he tried to stop me, I wouldn't listen. I get he isn't happy about this arrangement, but he could have said no. I take the dogs with me and head into the gas station, needing a few minutes alone and not breathing the same air as that dick. Taking my time, I pick out snacks and magazines before meeting him back in the car.

He sits facing forward in the driver's seat, not sparing me a glance, and starts the engine.

"You want me to drive?"

"No. Get your seatbelt on. We are wasting time."

"Then take me home."

"Harley, hurry the hell up." When I don't listen, his arm darts out and pulls the belt over my lap. It snaps into place, along with my temper. I seethe on the inside, and it spills over into my words. "Don't get near me again."

He stills and slowly faces me. "You would say that, but we both know what you are really pissed about. You need a hard fuck and know that I can deliver. Do yourself a favor and stop being such a spoiled bitch."

I blink.

Then I blink again, because in all honesty, I don't know when the last time, if ever, I have been called that. My walls go up and so does my resolve to keep his dick away from me. I may need a man, but not one as crass as this asshole.

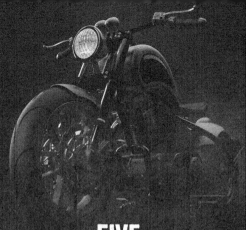

FIVE

Ice

The rest of the ride to Las Vegas gave me plenty of time to think. In fact, all I thought about was my revenge. Thank you, Axl, for that. It got my mind off all the ways I wish I could have Harley, up against the car, or in a gas station bathroom. The little momma's boy set me up on purpose. If we have the dogs, then what? I couldn't fuck his mom, or he did it just to make me miserable. Instead of reacting, I'm tucking this info away to use against him when I need it. Not today, but revenge will be served. I haven't made it this far by losing my cool. Game on, Axl.

At the MGM Grand, I park at the valet and help Harley and her dogs out. The heat is unbearable this time of year. Even in the shade, it cloaks over me like a sauna. She gets the dogs on leashes while I hand the valet her luggage. Several large bags for a few days when here I stand with one duffle bag slung over my shoulder. She leads us in through the front doors, and the swoosh of the door and air conditioning is welcoming. Do I give a rat's ass that she walks in front of me with two dogs? No. The few steps I am behind her, for one, gives me a great view of her ass, and two, I see every man's head turn to watch the gorgeous bombshell walk through the lobby, all of them thinking she belongs to me. Their heads turn away as soon as they catch my cold stare and clenched jaw. Deep down, I'm enjoying this little charade. It's wrong, no doubt. Her dead husband was my brother in the MC, but she's been freed from those ties, and that means Harley is available. Tasting her skin, hearing her moaning in pleasure, all these ideas run on as fantasies and I can't decide which one I'd pick to do first. On the other hand, I am here for a reason and that is to find and kill the man responsible for hunting down my brothers. Since we buried the Cartel King a few years back, it's been a mess to keep under wraps. ATF has been looking for him and is relentless in sending those of us who had any part in it to the Federal Penitentiary. These fuckers are like pit bulls with lockjaw on a fucking bone—they aren't letting this shit go.

Harley digs into her purse to pull out her wallet. I beat her to it and slap down my black Amex on the counter. Her eyes draw up to mine and I raise my eyebrows in response. I could care less about money, no way in hell would I allow her to pay. My hand touches her hip and I tug her close to whisper, "A man never allows a woman to pay. Not a word." Don't ask me where in the hell those words came from. I haven't been with a lady in so long. The dick in me wants to touch her, wants all these men to believe she's claimed, even though I would have never thought of myself settling down and having someone like her. Harley is a classy biker bitch. Someone like her is far and few in between. She is the end game, the one who rides at your back for life. For years, I have made no apologies and I'm not about to start either. I do what I want, and nothing in the end is too good for me if I want it.

Harley is a smart woman. She makes an ah-ha-ing noise, places a hand on my shoulder, and plays right along for a moment. I fight the smile that she almost pulled from me. Only problems come from that, so I tap it back down.

I need to keep my distance from her and not muddy the lines. Being so close to her after years at a distance is confusing. I only use women for one thing, anything more puts ideas in their heads. At the door, I swipe her card and walk in first, checking the rooms. She turns on the T.V. and I settle into my room.

We have joint rooms, but I insisted she leave the door between us unlocked. Some things never change and if I am here to protect and watch over her, I need complete access. Needing the space, the hours passed with no words said between us, only what I wanted for dinner. We eat alone when our food arrives. Only the sounds of the T.V. and her dogs running around breaks up the awkwardness.

Harley poked her head into my room and gently asked to walk the dogs before bed. For the life of me, I cannot figure out why anyone would want to deal with this shit on a regular basis. The extra task tempers my mood even further, but I take them to the spot designated for dogs. Harley needs her sleep, tomorrow she has a meeting with her old manager and a gang of publicists and I have my own work ahead of me, so I hurry along, much to her disapproval. The last few days of minimal sleep is wearing me down. On the way back to the room, I notice the change in her demeanor. The hotheaded temptress has left. She has fallen back in the company of demons, forgetting who she is and where she needs to be. It's none of business, so ignore her personal problems. I assume it has something to do with being back in Las Vegas. The sooner she realizes it's just a place, the quicker she can bounce back.

During the elevator ride, she looks ahead, trapped in her world. It's a damn shame. I know how to exorcise those demons and find the physical pain to help release the emotional, a connection with yourself so raw it's spiritual. I could pin her against the wall and take her to that place, but that would also mean she would belong to me—I would be responsible for her soul.

I can't do that to her. If I open that door, I can't shut it on her when I'm ready to go. Harley needs the bite of pain to release the temptation to taste death. Axl really doesn't see her suffering. Only a partner could, and I am not that man. The only thing I can offer is to lead her to safety inside our motel room, where we suffer alone.

It's impossible to lay here and sleep. The quiet pain is a distant friend we know all too well. I moved from the bed to a chair next to the door and waited. Harley hasn't stopped crying for a while. My mind has been at war with myself about what to do. The guilt creeps in at how I have treated her all day, like a job. But she is a job. Is it my problem? I know it's not, but she makes me second guess myself and that is unacceptable. I'm the coldest asshole out there. I will gut a man open without question, but the barest parts of her soul scare the shit out of me. That's why the bastard in me sits and hides in the dark. She'll harden up and be better for it.

Why can't I walk in there? Lend her an ounce of comfort? Because I gave up on kindness, love, any of that a long
time ago. It was easier to be free of it and live in the dark,
even now. I want to swallow my pride and be a better man,
but I never will be that young fool again. I don't know how.
Every tear that drips down her face is one that I wish I
could have. My hands would wipe them away and her pain
would become mine, giving her some peace. I couldn't af-
ford to be weak then and I refuse to be now, no matter how
much I crave her demons.

Eventually, she gives in and falls asleep. Quietly, I walk
into her room. Her dogs perk up but thankfully lay silently
back down against her. They cuddle Harley in her sleep,
protecting her from herself. The lights from outside dance
around the ceiling. Life is never-ending, but we trap our-
selves in the past.

Harley's face is beautiful and relaxed in her sleep. The
tears have stained her cheeks and no doubt will show tomorrow. Her pain draws me in like a beacon and I sit in
a chair across the room. Thoughts linger of what it would
be like to love a woman like her. Maddox had it all with
her at his side. He must have spent many nights watching
her like I am now. I can sense him with her and the level
of devotion they had to each other. The heady emotion is
causing my chest to crack open just barely enough to open
parts of me that should be left buried.

How someone so small can be so inspirational is in-
triguing. If I were Maddox all those years ago, I would have
stolen her light from the world for myself too. Men are
thieves, and we hold the world in our hands, where women
want to give it away and share it. For hours, I think about

the world and my place in it before I return to my room and let it all go. I am a killer and always will be.

Harley

It all came crashing down as soon as I slowed down. The past caught up with me quickly and memories of us resurfaced. Maddox and I met in Las Vegas and lived here for years raising Axl together. I fought against the anguish. Being here is almost too much. Axl was right to worry about me coming back. It's as if a different life happened here. I guess it was. At some point, I gave in and let the sadness wash over me. There is no holding on, only to go through it. I'm determined to remember Maddox and not cripple over in pain anymore.

I've been Battle Born for years, finally now understanding the concept. I gave in and stopped fighting to control what I was holding onto, the last thread tying me to the past. I ripped open the wound of the memories and felt them all. But now, I am ready to let go of what it was, what has happened, and be grateful I had him for the time I did. Thankfully, I have a piece of him in Axl and his daughter, the future Maddox has gifted me. It will always be hard, but I need to celebrate him and end the mourning.

Peeling the mask from my eyes, I get ready to head to the pool to relax. I opt for a messy bun and find Ice to let him know I want to go downstairs for some sun before the heat of the afternoon is here.

I knock on the entryway and he spins around. "I was going to catch some pool time. Would you want to go?"

"Harley?" He stalks closer to where I stand.

"Yes?" I emphasize, clueless about his antics.

"You better cover that ass before we leave. Fuck knows how many men I would have to kill on our way there and back. Grab a robe, woman!"

Wrapping myself up as best as possible with just my arms is fruitless. "What is wrong with my bathing suit? It is Vegas, Ice."

"That is not a fucking bathing suit. It's barely holding onto your body with strings. But you know what, let's go to the pool. I'm ready." He tucks his phone and keycard into his pockets and darts into the bathroom, coming out moments later, bringing two towels with him.

"They have towels at the pool, Ice!" I thunder at his back as he heads for the door. He doesn't listen and holds it open for me. Then he waves his hand impatiently, signaling for me to go ahead.

Anger washes over me and I am bound and determined to not care. Steam radiates off me on my way to the elevators.

Thankfully, a couple was just exiting and the doors remain open. Ice's cold exterior permeates the space and a chill runs up my spine. I jam my finger over the button for the pool, then cross my arms as the doors slide shut very slowly, flaring my anger even more.

Ice leans over. "Tell me, Harley, how secure would you feel, dressed like that, alone with a man like me?" His finger dances up my spine, the sharp intake of breath a clear signal and giveaway to my discomfort. My back locks up tight from his touch and the idea of an attacker snakes fear through me. My blood runs cold in my veins at the devil's words from behind me.

"Who's going to save you in this small space?" He hisses out through his teeth.

Ice is wound up tight, ready to strike. He's proved his point. I couldn't fight off a man, but I'm no coward either.

Slowly, I turn, the space between our chests nonexistent as my hard nipples brush his chest, and say, "I've been around many men just like you. You will not shame me to be different to make yourself feel more secure. I know I am a woman and a man could easily kill me. I also refuse to live in fear, and I'm not stupid. I will live, Ice, because at the end of it all, I want that. To be free. So don't try and hold me back. I'll listen and I'll be patient, but don't expect me to bow down and kiss your ass like your club girls."

Our scowls hold in a fight for dominance. We could tear each other down, leaving only shreds left. What will he choose? "I'm not going to treat you like a princess and hold you on a pedestal. You want to make a decision, then you handle those consequences. I'll back you up, but don't expect me to kiss *your ass* like you're used to. You want to go against me and fight me at every turn? Go the fuck ahead. I'll be the first to tell you, I told you so."

He pauses but keeps the hard glint in his eye. Lust laces the air we inhale. His tight and rigid posture tells me he is holding himself back. Every breath taken may as well be fire, my insides burn so hot. Nothing can be heard except the soft music playing in the background, a total contradiction to the atmosphere. The tornado of the battle we stirred holds strong until the elevator stops and the noise of machines on the floor filter in when the doors slide back open. Ice's large body is blocking off my view and exit. He stands his ground and challenges me to choose.

My hand darts out and rips the towel away from his hand. I wrap it around my body tautly. Now satisfied, he steps back and allows me to exit before him. I storm off, not remembering or caring where I was headed, just away from him. Ice's grip halts me and tugs me in the opposite direction. "Get your head together. The pool is this way."

Ripping my arm away, I blast through the double doors to the outside pool. Tearing the towel away from my body, I drop it onto a lounge chair, then dive into the pool. I wasn't going to swim, but suddenly I have a storm of feelings I need to exercise out. Ice is one stubborn, mean asshole who riles up my insides like I have never felt in my life.

Ice

I should have let her go to the pool by herself. For some reason, I couldn't let her leave in just scraps of fabric. Harley is an older woman, close to my age, and hot as fuck. I don't want to share her and that pissed me off. I took it out on her, but I didn't care either, because I got my way for the most part. I need her body tucked under mine for a few good hours to work out the tension that has grown between us in just twenty-four hours. She is begging me to take care of her and the only way she knows how to communicate is by being a brat. Harley needs a man, one with a firm hand and swift smack.

The pool boy is getting an eyeful of her tits. Harley has her arms laid across the pool deck and her head back, oblivious to his gaze on her. Her tits are bobbing and glistening just above the water. The polka dot red bikini is misleading as fuck. The woman was built for sin and deserves a man to take care of her. Not me. I don't do attachments and Harley is a part of the club. Hurting her would get me buried in a mineshaft.

The boy comes back to Earth and leaves her breakfast at a nearby table. He then politely informs her the food has been served and holds out a towel for her. Her smile catches the sun and his full attention as she pulls herself up and out of the water. Drops of water caress her skin, rolling down to the floor. She has a tan already, but Harley is glowing after a few hours in the sun. She thanks him and his cheeks pink before leaving. Harley ties the towel around herself and sits at the table.

"I love Vegas," some suit and tie schmuck comments next to me.

"Me too. Keep your eyes off her," I snarl and the bastard's face pales when he reads my cut, Royal Bastards MC. I wear it proudly.

My chair scrapes across the floor of the outside bar. Picking up my beer, I tap the top of his and walk away as the asshole has to chug to keep it from spilling over. In my jeans and cut, I strut across the distance and sit across from Harley. "You about done? It's getting too hot out here."

She has a piece of fruit on a fork she is taking a bite from, her luscious lips wrapped around the sweet fruit. My dick wants out and my mouth wants to claim those lips and taste how sweet she is. Why, I ask myself again, do I go there? If I take her the way I want, I will ruin her for other men. That idea makes me hard as a fucking boulder.

"Yes. I need to get ready to meet my old manager this afternoon. Also, I need to walk the dogs before we leave."

Those words mean nothing, but the 'we' coming from those hot lips sparks the already dissolving willpower I have left at not touching her. I nod and follow her out of the pool. On my way, I do make a point to scowl at the schmuck. I excel at being a dick.

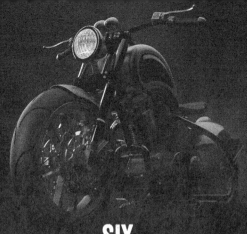

SIX

Harley

"How long has it been? I swear, girl, you could have been the next big thing. I hated it when you left modeling all those years ago." Carly, my old agent, straightens her suit jacket and walks over in her heels to give me a hug.

"It's been a long time, but my life was with Maddox and Axl. Nothing could've replaced that. But thank you for this opportunity. Can I introduce you to Ice?"

He holds out his hand, gives her a nod, and attempts a somewhat welcoming face. I chuckle and his cold eyes whip over to me. I place a hand on his other arm to calm down the beast always ready to fight. Earlier, it helped me to think while I was swimming that it wouldn't do me any good to poke at him. It would be a challenge he would gladly take on. I need to be smarter when dealing with the broody man. We are both just dealing with our own stress, why fight about stupid stuff? He is doing me a favor, and I forgot what it was like to be with a man like him, like Maddox. Being alone, I don't have someone to check in with anymore. It's an adjustment, one I will happily make.

Carly can't take her eyes off the two of us. I can see the wheels spinning and my mouth opens to correct her when Ice pulls out a chair for me. Carly clears her throat to sit down at the front of her desk, swallowing any personal questions she wanted to ask.

Shuffling a few papers around, she starts our meeting. "Okay, so we have a contract for the showcase this weekend." She hands me the document while rattling off a schedule. "We will have these photos of the show years ago on posters everywhere. Then we want to do a remake, a live shoot again, and finally, the auction. It was one of our best promotions."

She continues to go over the schedule of promotional shots that we need to take in the studio before the bike show. It becomes crystal clear why I ran away with Maddox when I could. I don't miss any of this. But it also occurs to me why I came. I needed space, a getaway from the person I have been hiding from the world. I changed. This was my way of getting away from my family, to find myself without their eyes. This trip was for me.

Ice clears his throat, signaling for me to pay attention, and it worked. "Okay, great." I try to politely cut off her rant. "Ice and I have another engagement. We will review the documents later. Thanks again, Carly." I stand and Ice gets up with me. I wonder if coming here was a mistake altogether. Ice isn't happy and I am not the young model I once was. That is crystal clear.

"Ah, Harley, there is a dinner tonight with the investors. Will your gentleman friend be joining you?"

Just like old times, she keeps me in line because she knows I would have blown that off.

For the first time, Ice speaks and it's not pleasant, more like a growl. "Who the hell else would be going, Carly?"

She bites the corner of her lip before responding, "Quite obviously my mistake. You would be, my apologies. See you both at Caesars, seven-thirty."

Before Ice can say anything else, I grab his stiff arm to lead him out the door. Once we reach the parking lot, I can't help but laugh out loud at his temper.

"Care to tell me what's so funny, Harley?"

"You are, and I am going to enjoy every minute of you in a suit. Looks like we are going shopping, sweetheart, since you made yourself my date tonight."

"I don't need clothes, Harley. I will wear what is already on my body."

"Then stay at the hotel."

"No"

"Then at least get a nice shirt."

"No."

"Then, no."

Ice's face grows bright red. He snatches the door handle with a fiery temper and whips the door open.

"Thank you, honey." I hop in and smile his way.

His scowl says he's not amused and proves my point when he slams the door in my face. I laugh the entire way as he walks around the car and until his large body is in. The car is started and he punches the gas, driving down the highway.

Ice

Why in the hell is this so funny? Still, she keeps her hackles up as I speed toward the mall. The mall—a place where I do not belong. Parking the SUV outside of Macy's, I take a glance at Harley from the corner of my eye. The woman waits me out.

"If you make a big deal about this, I'll make sure neither one of us leaves the hotel room tonight," I threaten, but the lightness in her eyes tells me she doesn't see me as a threat.

"Absolutely not. Let's grab some lunch too. We can make it a date day." She jumps out and waves me out to join her. Sometime between last night to now, Harley kicked off whatever was weighing her down. She has found a way to come alive, and in turn has taken me down a road I have never been. I haven't dated in over twenty years and have never gone to the mall with any woman in my life.

The oddity of the normal gestures and her sweetness has chipped away at the ice around my heart. It has to be the perfect mix of defunction we are together, sweet and spicy. Taking a deep breath, I steal myself the possibilities that will never be mine. Her words and actions mean nothing. I have never allowed myself the luxury of a commitment. The idea of it seems out of my grasp and too much. I've never thought of it as a positive. It always felt like extra work. But she makes me believe there are positives, ones I don't want and toss away out of my mind. The devil requires his dues, and I'm here to handle club business and collect.

She falls into step with me, snaking her hand at my elbow, lightly holding on. The warmth of her body heats up mine in ways I have never felt, and I again remind myself she's not looking for what I want, a dirty, hard fuck. Friends with benefits at best. She deserves more than the man I am. My attendance at this meeting tonight is important, not for Harley, but for the clubs. I need the names of the men investing in the shoot.

"You okay?" Harley bumps my shoulder with hers and squeezes my arm. "We really don't have to go tonight. What are they going to do? Fire me? Who cares? Then we could just hang out."

"It's fine." If I say anything, could she read into how much I want her? I couldn't risk that and be too insistent we go to this dinner.

"Well, this is a first. I haven't had a date in years. Thank you for coming with me."

"You haven't dated since Maddox?" What I am really wondering is, who has she slept with.

"Nope," she pops. "I'm in a great place for once. I want to keep things easy. I want to live and feel happy. I didn't live for a long time after he passed."

I stop abruptly. My eyes search hers for any tell that she could be lying. Harley's eyes are sincere and soft. Deep inside, she has a lingering pain only the loss of someone you love would leave. A crazy, animalistic, possessive feeling tugs at my gut. She hasn't given herself to anyone else. I have no other choice but to take her. The addiction is real and there is no extinguishing it. I will taste her before another man can touch her.

"You're a good woman, Harley. Never settle for

anything less than you deserve." Which means, stay far away from men like me, who want to devour her beauty for themselves, stealing it to make themselves better.

Her hand touches my cheek. "Ice, you are a better man than you give yourself credit for."

Surprisingly, Harley reads me easily and her simple touch is genuine, turning my stomach into knots. "C'mon. I need to find a black shirt." The desire to take her lips is pumping through my veins. We both need a distraction and I keep us in stride through the doors.

"What about a dark blue?" she asks and places her hand back into my arm.

Raising a brow, I question her without words. "It would match your eyes." Harley winks and leads me inside the store. I've never bought a collared shirt. Never had a reason to care or to wear one. She doesn't ask or make a big deal about it, but finds a sales associate to take my measurements. Harley picks out the color she wants to see me wear—and I let her. For once in my life, I trust a woman. Even if it is just a shirt, I let her do it for me.

Being here, alone in Las Vegas, it feels like I can be a different person and no one will see. Maybe, I can hide the demons that play at the surface and a past that doesn't exist. I can pretend to be a different man, a man who is worthy of a woman like her.

After lunch and then a frozen yogurt, she takes me on a tour through the Strip and places she used to haunt. I've seen the Strip, at night, but not places she's been to. I go along for the ride. Seeing life through her eyes is an interesting adventure and relaxing. I listen to all her stories. What I hear is she loved her husband. Also, Harley is ready for new memories. Another chapter awaits her, and some lucky bastard will be at her side.

"Is there anywhere you want to go?" she asks. What she really wants is for me to give her the same tour into my life. She doesn't want to see this place the same way I have.

I think over her question anyway. The cold hard truth is, I want to consume her. Devour her body and pain that she holds inside and free it. I know how to do it, but we would never come back the same from it if I do. My brothers would probably kill me for what I want to do with her. We both would benefit from it, but I can't "go" there with this woman. I can't show her what it is like to orgasm while my grip almost takes the life from her, so she can release the fear of the question she wants answered most—what is death like?

"No. You need to get ready." I'm a coward, or could I be a smart man having restraint? I think the latter and walk away without words. It hurts her. I can see it in her eyes as they dart around the sidewalk outside of the MGM Grand. Harley doesn't spend time with people who don't make her comfortable with reassurances and kind gestures. I get it. Who wouldn't want to be that way with her? I can't. It's better this way. If she lets me in once, she'll be mine until I release her. I don't want her to be one of them, where I take it all until I find another one I want to play with.

While we were gone, I had a dog walker come up and take care of the dogs. As soon as we walk into the room, she finds them asleep and is concerned they are not more energetic. "A dog walker took them for the afternoon.

They will be back after we leave to take them back to the dog park. I'm going to take a shower." I don't need to see the happy, content smile from her and hurriedly walk away. I did it for her because she couldn't. It's quicksand I'm playing in. If we keep this up, we will be buried with no chance of coming out unscathed.

SEVEN

Harley

He stuns me.

I will admit that I never know what to expect from Ice. What he did, taking care of Bella and Ben, my dogs, was over the top sweet and so thoughtful. While I shower, dress, and get ready, I think about Ice and what I know about him. Everything I do know is limited. The guys don't talk about him much. For the most part, Ice keeps to himself. He comes across as cold and unyielding. I think it is true—he is cold and very forward.

The memories pop up of the times I have been around him. One in particular comes to mind, the last time I was here for Emilia and Cuervo's wedding. It was the stare we held when he was watching me. Those piercing blue eyes held so much more emotion in them than I had ever seen. Now, I wonder why he was looking at me that way. At the time, it was easy to dismiss because I was too distracted by the circumstances. I believe he has so much more underneath it all. Ice would no doubt kill a man, but I also feel he would be loyal to a woman if he could believe in himself. I would venture to guess he was never given the opportunity to love. That makes my heart sad for him. There is so much more there for him, if only he could see it. I hope someday, someone lights his world on fire and his walls go up in flames.

My mind wanders off, thinking about his harsh touch and the commanding tone he delivers when he demands attention. My skin tingles remembering the power in his touch. Exhaling audibly, I chastise myself. Ice doesn't keep his women long. He would eat me alive and leave me wrung out. I want it, to taste every inch of what he has to offer, but it comes with an expiration date. One I need to remember. Ice isn't forever, and only has a good time for right now.

I still with the make-up in my hand. What am I thinking? How could I even? Should I feel bad? It's been so long since my husband has laid a hand on me that I miss it. I miss feeling loved, the passion, and now I miss him. Except it is confusing. I miss the intimacy and love I shared with my husband, but Ice has started to take that place. I crave the raw desire between two people, communicating with a look or gesture. Setting the lipstick on the counter, I walk over to the glass window, my black heels sinking into the carpet with each step.

Running my hands up my arms, I start talking to Maddox. "I wish you were here. I miss your voice and words, my best friend. Our time was up, and I would do anything to do it all over again, but we can't. What I haven't figured out is how to move forward. I want to, but the guilt stops me—"

"He wouldn't want you wasting your time." Ice's deep baritone shocks me and I dart my gaze to find him in his black jeans and dark blue shirt, watching me from behind. That stare is the same one I saw at the wedding not too long ago. "Maddox wouldn't want you to waste any part of your life. He would live full throttle. There is a difference between betrayal, loyalty, and remembrance. What you are doing is sacrificing your life, killing your heart. You are ready, Harley. Take the next jump."

Hard and deep breaths leave my lungs. A zing of lust courses through my muscles and my throat is tight. Anticipation is thick in the air. Ice walks forward until his chest brushes against my back, his fingertips feather softly across the skin on my arms. "Why is it such a sin to be happy? Do what your body tells you, what you are ready for. Let your mind be free of the consequences." He leans in to tell me more but holds the words close to his chest. His touch falls away, leaving me on edge.

My resolve is almost washed away. There in the window, I can see his reflection, see his soul, and what is lurking behind the rough exterior. I turn to him, to beg him to tell me more, to not stop, but he holds his arm out. "It's time to go to dinner."

I want to scream at him. Why? Why are you making me crazy? But I don't. I take his offered arm, and like a fool, I follow the cold-hearted bastard out the door.

Ice

Harley doesn't see my pain, the agony my body feels from holding back. I want nothing more than to peel the black dress from her body and taste her sinful salty skin. I don't give in and do what I know will hurt her. I want better for her. She deserves more than I can give—I only take.

While she is with me, no one will even attempt to try. At the upscale casino restaurant, I pull out her chair. Hungry eyes from the investors prey over her like a purchase or acquisition. She is much more than that, and my hard-set demeanor lets them know that. I would kill to keep her safe. I don't shake hands when the introductions are made. I could give a fuck about the size of their billfolds tucked away in their coat pockets.

They politely brush it off and I roll up my sleeves, showcasing my tattoos and gauging their reactions. From that point, they ignore me like the tools they truly are. They call on guys like me when life gets real dirty, someone to make the hard calls and keep their hands clean from the blood. Pussies.

Harley is polite, and again, whether she realizes she does it or not, she reaches out for me. Her hand either lands on my arm or thigh while she talks and eats through dinner. She shows composure and grace. What the rest don't see is how many times she rubs her legs together when she switches one over the other. Poor Harley needs assistance. If she were mine, I would have taken care of her desires and calmed her down with my face between her legs. She would know, without doubt, who her man is.

Reaching back, I place one arm on the back of her chair and to the other arm on the one to my left, fully exposing my body to the table. Dominance is a gesture. Carly, her old manager, can barely keep her eyes from roaming over the muscles packed under the stuffy shirt I put on for Harley. Naturally, she folds into my body like a magnet, like she fits here, and rests her hand on my leg. The position gives the appearance to the table that she is mine. To an extent, she is, or she could be. Harley needs a dominant man to lead. It sets her free. And since the death of her husband, she's been floundering and not understanding why.

I know who I am, and while they talk, I wonder if I should expose Harley to her true nature. My dick agrees with that idea, but it could cost more than what it's worth, So I decide against entangling our relationship any further. I could hurt her and the club in the long run, but I won't stop myself from enjoying her company. Minus the assholes at the table with us. I force myself to focus on the investors and the one who is baiting Harley.

"So, tomorrow at nine a.m., we will have our first shoot. Please bring your contract with you. We would also love to have you with us, Ice." Carly smiles and says goodbye.

First thing Carly is going to find out tomorrow before the shoot is that Harley isn't signing the documents until the percentage of her pay is adjusted. They lowballed her. They brought her back for a reason, and after some research, I found that they need her. She was a media stunt to pull in the crowds that have dwindled down over the years. That's worth more than the entry level contract they gave her. I doubt Carly knows how she played Harley into the hands of the sharks. I would put money on it that they asked for her specifically.

"We will see you tomorrow, Carly. Can I have your card? In case I need to contact you." Her face is temporarily stunned before reaching into her purse and handing me her card. I scowl her way and take it. She knows she will be hearing from me.

"On that note," an investor, Brian or some douchey name like that, mentions, "Harley, please take my card." He holds it between two fingers toward her. Harley moves to take the card, but I snatch it from him. She laughs to break the tension, thanking me, then tells the table goodnight. As she gets up, I wait a moment and when her back is turned, I toss the card back, flicking it Brian's way. It hits his chest and then the floor.

I want to howl at the moon. These men are not men at all. In any other clubhouse in the world, a fight would break out and someone would end up with a knife in the skull. Brian is the rat, I'm sure of it. He is the one we've been searching for, the investor helping the cartel before and now feeding the ATF. Brian had an alias while working with the cartel. I came down to get a picture to match it to the grainy ones. Every man who sat in those cartel meetings are now dead. If he is the same man, then he will be the last man to die, setting us free of the mess that has taken years to clean up. I have a long night ahead, calls will be made, then plans set into motion.

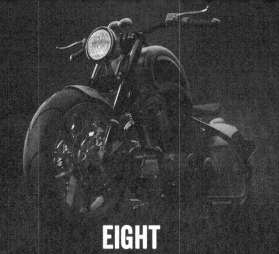

EIGHT

Harley

Holy hell, Ice is smokin' hot and I need to climb him like a tree in the elevator. I hold myself together, just barely. He commanded that dinner like a god or the devil. He didn't have to say a word and had everyone's attention. I would fan myself if I wouldn't look like such a fool. If he were wearing a tie, I would drag him straight to my bed.

The elevator door dings and it breaks me free from my daydreams of having his face between my legs. His hard dick in my mouth. I could go on and on. My face feels hot and my skin breaks out in a sweat. Inside my hotel room, I grab a small bottle from the mini bar and take a shot. Leaning forward, I rest my hands on the table, trying to ignore the pulsating need demanding attention. Ice's expert attention and care is desired. His words from earlier mixed with his touch throughout dinner is a potent cocktail. It lit a fuse that isn't willing to be put out.

Ice is good at hiding what he doesn't want others to see. I could see his intent and sense it deep in my bones. We can't hide the physical need anymore. We've been playing a game of cat and mouse, neither one of us wanting to pull the trigger. I was slow to the game, but I see it now. Question is, do I want to go for it? The answer is yes. There is only one thing I need to sate my desire and that is an orgasm from that man.

Decision made. I turn and am not surprised to find Ice and his hooded eyes watching me. "Your next move could change a lot of things. Make sure it is me you want to do this with, Harley. I'm not an easy man, not what you are used to." He waits patiently for my answer, but I have no words. Just my raw, unbridled desire to offer.

My hands run down my sides to the hem of the black dress. Slowly, I pull it up and over my head. The fabric lifts away and my hair floats around my shoulders and face. My breasts heave and my nipples grow hard. The dress falls to the floor, discarded along with any doubt. I stand in front of Ice in a black lace thong and heels. Tiptoeing to him, I feather my touch over his chest. "What is it you want from me, Ice?" I hiss, sounding out the "s".

His heart is thundering underneath my palms. "Lay on the bed, Harley, and spread your legs wide for me. I'll give you what you are asking for tonight. It will only ever be one night."

"Why not while we are here," I taunt.

Like a snake, he strikes and has a fistful of my hair. "I can only hold back one time." He runs his nose from my collar up to my ear to snarl, "After tonight, if you tease me again, you will get it harder than you have ever had in your life. I can guarantee you that. Go." He lightly lets go, his warning clear. He wants it rough and dirty and that makes me curious and hot all at the same time.

ICE

Sauntering over to my room, I leave the door open. Standing in front of my bed, I drop my panties. Spinning around, I catch the predator I know him to be, soaking in every detail of my flesh. Gracefully, I sit back on the bed, bringing my feet up, and I scoot back just a bit. I lay back and catch a glimpse of his dark clothing coming my direction. Spreading my legs apart, I showcase what hasn't been touched by a man in years. Keeping my focus on him, I wait.

Ice unbuttons his shirt and tosses it aside, then comes to stand over me at the end of the bed. He reaches for my calf and lifts my leg up. Removing the first shoe, he begins to massage my foot. My mind goes numb, my eyes shutting and a loud moan escaping. He takes his time, learning every point of my body that craves the most attention. Strong hands massage my calf and thigh muscles. Ice kisses the inside of my ankle and follows a line down to my knee, nipping my skin in various spots. My audible gasps please him because they are followed by a kiss every time.

He does the same to my other leg, the tenderness completely relaxing me. Fingers glide up my sides until they reach my breasts. I can't look away from him. Ice is so strong and powerful, but with me, he shows mercy. The bed dips with his weight next to me. I want to touch his entire body like he's doing to mine. It's a sweet deliverance from hell. Ice sees me reach for him but stops me, taking my hands in his and positioning them over my head. His message is clear. I am not allowed to touch. Why?

An unspoken rule is set, he leads and delivers. I am there to take what he gives without question. What surprises me most of all is I want it. No, need it. Ice kissed every inch of my body, but not my lips. He leaves those untouched and it doesn't go unnoticed by me.

I cannot complain and get lost in his touch anyway. Each stroke of his tongue, especially when he finds my hard-aching nipples, is a deal signed by the devil. He licks, sucks, then blows cool air over them. The hot and cold sensation makes me rock my body, silently begging him to deliver me to the finish line.

Ice plays with me like he is tuning up his bike—with care and experience. Every touch and caress is to warm up my body, but I am way past that. I am ready to boil over and combust from the heat radiating off our bodies. My eyes clench tight as I pant for him and will him to take his cock out and give it to me as hard as he promised. Ice has brought my body back to life and finding the vixen inside who wants to be freed.

He nips and kisses a straight line down from my stomach to my pussy. Once there, he delivers a sensual kiss to my clit. Ice inhales me and groans out his pleasure this time. I don't move and my muscles relax into the mattress when Ice opens his mouth and takes a long lick before devouring me like a starving man. He is relentless in his pursuit to bring me to orgasm and doesn't stop until he is satisfied after I come twice with his tongue on me and his fingers inside me.

NINE

Ice

What I did last night was a warm-up for Harley of what it could be like. She needed to know that she is still a woman, with or without her husband. Sex is not bad for her, and in fact, she craves it, with the right partner. I wanted to give her what she needed first. I craved to fuck her raw and dirty after she came for me. I wanted to drive my cock into her so hard, she would come alive for only me and remember whose dick gave her one of the best nights of her life.

But I knew if I did, it would send the wrong message to her. She is a woman to keep at home like a queen, locked away for your own dirty deeds. Men will wonder, and only you know what she tastes like. I'm not a man who keeps a woman. I toss them aside before they get attached. The new girls who will take my dick like I need, I keep from the brothers at first. I don't share, ever.

Instead of feeding my needs, I left Harley alone and sated in bed to go take a shower, coming hard in my hand to relieve the tension in my balls. Jacking off again this

SCARLETT BLACK

morning is not enough to kill the need rooted deep in my balls. The taste of her is a drug that captures a man and chains him to her. For most men, that would be a gold-mine, but for me, it isn't.

While Harley is sleeping in, I make a call to Carly and give her a piece of my mind. "I will guaran-fuckin-tee you will have a presence of bikers at your show. That's why you called her after all. Bring her pay up thirty percent or no deal. She doesn't need this shit of jumping through hoops. The woman has had enough."

Carly doesn't argue, but her gritted response tells me she knew Harley wouldn't argue and that shit pisses me the fuck off. If I have my say, she will never waste her time dealing with assholes again. I get why she's here. Harley is bored at home and wasting away. It's time she opens her eyes and stops being so blind. Next, I call Grim, the Prez of the Vegas and Tonopah Royal Bastards MC. They will be ready to ride in for the event. Then I call Diesel from the Flagstaff Royal Bastards to confirm his presence. All the surrounding clubs will be here this weekend.

A few more calls and markers are paid to have a pres-ence at the show, all to make her feel like the queen she is. Maybe it's my guilt that forces me to make it right, but I don't spend too much time analyzing it. She will be getting a fat payday that she can play with and never come back. In fact, I hate the idea of pictures being taken of her and all the men who will whistle for her. Want her. On the other hand, she needs it. Needs to feel for herself that she is still sexy as fuck, even though she is a grandmother. That—is funny as hell. No one would believe that if they took one look at her. I wouldn't even believe she was a mother.

Speaking of the devil, my phone rings with an incoming call from Axl. "Yeah," I answer curtly.

"Why isn't my mom answering her phone?"

"Why, you need your mommy?"

"Fuck you, Ice. I want to give her an update on Blade and Vegas's baby girl."

"She's sleeping in. We had a late night." I hold back the laugh that wants to be let loose when he starts flipping his shit, cursing and threatening to chop off my dick for touching her. "It's none of your damn business what your mom does or doesn't do. Quit treating her like glass and let her live, for fuck's sake. Do you really want her to be a grandmother and live like one, you selfish prick?"

Axl growls over the line, "I'll see you when you get back." The line drops. I get it. He thinks he has to protect her. But he doesn't. He needs to give her some space and let her learn to walk on her own two feet.

Sitting at the table, I hear her start the shower and a pang of disappointment hits me. I would rather be inside her, or inside the shower with her this morning. Like everything else on this messed up trip, I push it aside. It isn't going to happen, and I need to come to that understanding now.

Her dog, I think Bella, comes over to whine at my feet. Her little paws pad at my pants and she begs for me to pick her up. She is persistent in her pursuit for attention. I even try to nudge her away while I work, but she sits there, shaking her tail and pawing at me.

"I think she likes you," Harley comments, coming into my room.

I grunt in response because, really, it doesn't know

anything besides begging for food or affection. She picks her up, giving her what she wanted, attention. Ben naps and ignores the room. That dog gets it, minds his own damn business. Harley sits across from me and starts picking at the breakfast I ordered, not in a hurry to get anywhere. I look at my watch, but she ignores the cue to move it along. I'm moody and can't shake off my irritation this morning.

"Are you not getting ready?" It takes at least an hour before she can walk out the door to go anywhere. I can't handle being late to anything. Harley sitting and enjoying her breakfast means she will be late.

"No. They do my hair and makeup there. They tell me what to wear. All I need to do is show up," she explains easily.

"Then at least put some clothes on your body," I grit out. The bathrobe hanging off her shoulder is exposing more than she should.

"Ice," she calls, watching my gaze run over her body. My cock twitches, wanting more. The call to connect with her is so strong, I don't know if I can make it another couple of days and not be inside her.

When I meet her stare, she grins. "It was a one-time thing, or are you planning what I am? Three more days to explore what this is, then we go home and never talk about it again? What happens in Vegas…" Harley raises from her chair to walk away. Over her shoulder, she leaves one last thought between us, "You know where to find me if you do."

She is a million-dollar model.

The golden bikini looks like latex painted on her skin. They dusted her body with some gold glitter. A true biker garage calendar fantasy came to life before my eyes. Desire to ruin it all with every touch from me becomes my addiction. Thirty minutes have passed while I stand guard in the corner. It has only gotten harder by the minute, my dick included.

Harley's promise to have her for three days becomes a bargain too hard to pass up. I weigh and measure the outcome. Could I do my job and have her too? If I piss off Battle Born, what would that do to our ties? Hard to say. There is a code—we don't mess around with Ol' Ladies, but technically, she's not an Ol' Lady anymore.

My phone vibrates with a text from Diesel.

Diesel: Info is confirmed.

Meaning Brian is our rat and the target for me to take out before he digs any deeper, taking information back to the ATF. It is my job to find him and take him out without suspicion. It has to be undetected, even by Harley, and a thought comes to mind of how I can make it all work. This will all be a little too easy. I get to work making necessary local connections while the sounds of the camera's flash goes off behind me.

TEN

Harley

Maybe I read the situation all wrong. I thought for sure I could get him sold on a fling in Vegas. Especially when I came out dressed like a goddess in gold. Ice was distracted with his phone and busy with what appears to be texting. I can't lie and say I wasn't looking forward to a little flirting. It is better that I'm not distracted, get my head back into work, and forget he is in the background of the shoot.

Several changes and props later, I am done and wiped out. A hamburger and a beer are calling my name. I need some rest before tomorrow's big day at the showcase and I'm dying to find out how this arranged marriage in my mafia book will work out.

Stepping out of the dressing room, I find an annoyed Ice. "Are you ready for some food?" I try to be friendly. If we are going to be here, we can at least make the best of it. Forget the mind-blowing orgasms he gave me with that mouth. Forget the feel of his body on mine. Yeah, I don't know that I will forget anything any time soon.

"Aye, let's get back to the room." Ice places a hand at the small of my back. Being next to him makes me feel delicate and small. I want to see what it would be like to have all of him, the real Ice under the man he allows everyone to see. I want to experience the darkness and power behind those eyes and muscles.

"Harley." Ice's deep baritone vibrates through his throat.

My eyes flutter and I regain my thoughts. "Yeah?"

"That golden bikini was hot as fuck."

Stunned by his words and compliment, it takes me a moment to find my voice. "It is a hot number. It made me feel alive."

Ice swats my ass and holds the door open for me to get in. "Pretty fucking hot and alive if you ask me." Like a gentleman, he shuts my door then gets into the driver's seat. He may as well take me to hell, because if he asked, I don't think I could tell him no.

I know from the whisperings at the club he's done some dark stuff. How dark, I'm not sure and really don't care. It's hard for me to picture any of these men as anything other than what we experience, But I'm not delusional about what they do. With the recurring violence and corruption, I can't find it in me to care. What is important is what life is like inside the four walls of my home. Ice is right—I was protected from the worst of it. I am different. My eyes are more open to it now, where before I ignored it all.

I've grown into a person I have yet to understand fully. I found another layer of myself I didn't know existed and is dying to be set free.

"What is it, Harley? I can hear you thinking."

"You." I hesitate with the truth on the tip of my tongue. "You make me want to see what the darkness is like. How far I can go and come back. I want you. To see what it is like to experience the darkness. Share in the depravity. I can't even explain the feeling, but you call to me."

Ice's stare stays on the road until we hit a stop light. "You need to understand something. I'm not going to buy you flowers and ask you on a date. I fuck, Harley. When I'm done, it's over, no questions asked. You need to remember that."

His hard gaze holds mine. The determination and resolve in his voice is hard not to understand. Ice doesn't give much of himself, the core of him, he trusts no one. "I'm not looking for love or flowers, just the experience to fly."

A car horn blares behind us and he looks ahead before hitting the gas. "Then understand, for three nights, your body belongs to me at will." His forearm muscle bulges with his grip on the steering wheel and I gulp back the lust. My fingers want to wind themselves around the muscles and veins.

Gone are any ideas of an easy night of relaxation. My body hums with anticipation and need. Dark fantasies I never knew existed come to mind and, suddenly, I wish we were alone back in the room. Pulling up to the valet, he tosses them the keys, his long strides through the lobby difficult for me to keep up with.

I'm out of breath by the time we reach the elevator. The doors close and his grip is ruthless in my hair. He drags me to him. My scalp is on fire and so is my body.

My fingers are digging into his shoulders. One leg wraps around his upper thigh. At the same time, his mouth devours mine while he tilts my head up to him.

My hips are grinding into his dick. Ice groans into my mouth, nipping at my lips, and his fingers dig into my ass. Picking me up, my other leg wraps around him. He charges forward until we slam into the wall. My fingers pull at his hair until the sound of the ping and the elevator doors open.

He lets me go but drags me along to our room. The dogs bounce up and down with excitement to see me. Ice is on a mission and shouts, "Quiet!" He will not be deterred, and I couldn't agree more. They whimper and lay down. I'm too far gone to care.

Once the door is slammed shut, he follows me into my room where I tug off my tank and push down my shorts. Ice tosses his cut and shirt onto a nearby chair. We collide in the middle of the room where he rips my bra and underwear away from my body. "No more games, Harley. Stand next to the window."

Peeling myself away, I walk to the window and gaze out at the city. "Place your hands above your head on the glass," he demands and I comply like it's my new favorite task. My heart is skipping every other beat with excitement. I'm not exposed with the privacy glass, but there is an illusion that I am with my naked body pressed against it. Ice taps my legs apart. Giving him it all, I push my ass toward him. Silently, I beg for him, wanting it all.

The sound of his belt unbuckling fills the air and my anticipation grows. The woosh of his belt lets me know it was hastily pulled from the loops of his pants. My mind pictures him standing behind me shirtless with his v on full display. "Do you like the bite of leather?" He rasps into my ear, "Or something more intimate? The sting of my hand?" The leather is traced up my side.

My breaths become labored and I want to curl further into every touch. "I'm going to start you off soft and build up to it." He continues to run the belt over my back, thighs, and arms. "Relax your muscles and let your mind take you away." Ice reaches around me and cups my breast, increasing the pressure then rolling and pulling on one nipple, then the other. My head falls back onto his shoulder. My arms shake, wanting to touch him, but I know I am not to move until he says to.

Ice glides his touch down to my pussy where he cups me before sliding his fingers into my folds. "You're excited for what comes next, aren't you, Harley?"

"Yes."

Pulling his fingers out, he drags the belt up my thighs and lightly taps my outer thighs then up my sides and arms. I wait for the sting of it, but it hasn't come yet. Only pleasure from each one. I crave more. I want to dive in deep with Ice, but wait, I want it all and don't want to miss a moment.

Each slap of the leather starts to gradually increase. The intensity is raw. A fire starts to build so bright inside, something so spiritual that belongs to me and me alone. Pent up frustration and doubt start to surface. Name it, I feel it—loneliness, regret, pain, each bite of the belt opening them as if they could bleed. The pain from the belt gets stronger. It's almost too much, until it hits the floor and my emotions explode before evaporating around me.

It all stops except the tornado of lust brewing inside. I'm not done, I need more. The protest almost leaves my lips, but Ice is there. His touch roaming over my flesh. His dick rubbing into my ass. Everything is a blur, and at some point, he brought me back. Ice grinds his steel dick into me. His nails digging into my hips. Ice rears back before plunging into me. One thrust and he is balls deep. My pussy clenching for the first time around him.

"Hold on." Ice isn't kind or romantic. He fucks me like he said he would. Every thrust is hard and aggressive. My legs tremble underneath me and my arms start to give way. Ice pulls out then whips me around. Picking me up and pushing forward fucking me against the glass. He is relentless in his pursuit to destroy my body.

Ice groans and his head falls back before snapping forward. The maniac lustful gaze makes my pussy clench. He hisses and his hand wraps around my throat. I moan into his touch. His teeth scrape across my lower lip, choking me harder, pistoning into me. I start to see stars and the building of pressure inside explodes. He releases his grip and I almost faint from the rush.

Ice nips at my neck and groans coming into his condom. Reality starts to seep in, and the cool glass is comforting at my back. He carries me to the bed and lays me down, tossing the covers over me. I hate the loss of his body, heat, and touch. Too tired and too spent, I sleep like I never have before, like the dead. Ice exorcised my demons and slayed me all at the same time.

ELEVEN

Ice

It doesn't take much to go unnoticed by the public. Details are forgotten as drinks are passed and flashy women parade around. Vegas is a hotspot for crime and makes a perfect setting to blend in easily.

Earlier, Harley gave the dogs a treat. Ruffling through her stuff, I find them and the dogs eagerly take the snacks and remain quiet. Standing, I check my pockets once again that I have everything I need, my cell, gun, knife, and keycard.

I leave my cut behind and opt for a long sleeve t-shirt and a baseball cap. Three blocks over is where Brian, the rat, is staying and it's time I do a stakeout. I know he had a meet planned with his ATF handler. Whatever information he passes along to him, I need to intercept, which will be bloody.

It's not a bar they meet at. It's where all the big bets are placed. Huge screens line the walls with horse races, boxing, and sporting events. The room is in the back of the casino floor. Men of all varieties litter the area, from expensive suits to the neighborhood guy who will probably lose his house and wife from the second mortgage he will need to pay off his habit.

I grab a card and find a seat at the back of the smoky dark room. A waitress comes by and sweetly takes my order for a beer. She scampers off, filling her bar orders, and I keep my eyes on her. She could be hired to do more than order drinks. Under the table, she may work for someone else, reporting the men who sit down. Could be someone as far up the food chain like the ATF, or her lousy boyfriend robbing winners in the parking lot.

She walks over to the bartender, handing off her ticket then counting her tips before pocketing them. Looking at her closely, she is tired and has a tattered top and pants on. I would bet she works two jobs and has a kid at home to feed. Forgetting her as a person to watch, I scan the room for faces. I'm early, Brian isn't due here for another thirty minutes. He won't turn up early, but the man in nondescript clothing and determination in his eyes tells me I found the ATF agent.

Looking at my card, I start to scribble down my bets and point spreads, taking my time while we wait for Brian to show up. My beer comes and I appear as if I'm watching the baseball game on the screen. After I finish my drink, I turn in my card to the cashier and hand over my cash to place my bet.

Where the ATF agent sits is a long table with dividers. The one second to the end is open and I take a seat. Brian shows shortly after and has a nervous habit of looking around. He's so uncomfortable, the agent slaps a hand on his shoulder to have a seat.

A few seconds into their conversation, Brian tells him Harley is in town but Blade and his chapter isn't anywhere near her or Stryker. The snitch does inform him I'm here and that ties me to their club, which is not good. Everything we have done will start to slowly unravel.

The agent tells him how important it is to have Harley alone before she leaves town. As we all thought, they are targeting her, hoping to get a window to leak out information for their case. She may not intentionally harm the MC, but any details could give them a bread crumb. She may not be as involved as before, but she'll always have to watch her back, and we'll be here to help. Once you're in the Club, you're in for life.

Their update isn't long because their informant doesn't have much, but the death toll has been increased to one more. The agent only has minutes left on this earth. My brain amps up in anticipation of how I am going to pull this off. This will be turned over to his commander within the hour and I don't have much time to plan.

With the cameras in the building, I have to be careful to not be caught following him. He's not going to risk being seen either. It's now or never. My body starts to hum at the chase to hunt him down, rapidly going over scenarios, keeping my focus on him and survival. I'll be going down as well as my club if I fail. I won't fail. I never do.

The agent leaves a few minutes after Brian. Staying on the opposite end of the casino floor, I recognize his exit strategy, through the side parking lot where locals usually park. I dart right and head through the long stream of restaurants, dodging the tourists and partygoers. I want one thing, to kill the agent before the call is made.

ICE

Passing a cart with souvenirs, I swipe a large hoodie from it in one fluid motion. As I approach a corner, I shove both arms in, holding onto the hat with one hand. I pull the hoodie over my head and slide the hat back on and pull the hood on top of the hat. My legs move with purpose and swiftly I find myself approaching the ATF agent in the back parking lot.

Keeping my head down, I charge him from behind like a fucking bull. He holds his phone in his hand, walking toward his car. With all my muscle, I shove him onto his own car and his phone clatters to the pavement. Lifting my boot, I stomp down and shatter the device into pieces. From my boot, I remove the blade and bury it into his back, one lung and then the other. He falls, gasping and choking on blood.

A woman screams off in the distance and I know my time is up. I grab his wallet and run like a mugger haphazardly around cars and eventually into the alleyways and deep into the city. Lost among the masses. I clean my blade that I tucked into the front pocket as much as possible and place it into my boot. Las Vegas never cools off. By the time I'm in the clear, I'm drenched with sweat. There is a dumpster and I toss the sweatshirt inside. The lid slams shut and I continue with my speed-walk back to the hotel where I left Harley.

It takes me thirty minutes by the time I silently slip through the door of our hotel room. Her dogs sound off like a damn alarm. Taking a tentative step, I think about choking the little bastards, but a light flips on. Harley stands in her room's doorway with a concerned look on her face.

TWELVE

Harley

Bella and Ben start to bark, waking me from a deep sleep. My heart leaps and my throat is tight with fear. I'm all alone, and for the briefest moment, I can't remember where I am. At first, I think I'm home, but quickly it all comes back to me.

The dogs haven't barked the entire time we've been here. Slowly, I get up from the bed. Pulling my phone from the nightstand, I carefully walk to the doorway and flick the light on once I recognize Ice is at the door. I want to say his appearance alarms me, but it doesn't. He doesn't have the face of a man who's been out drinking and sleeping around. He seems cool, but his shoulders are high and back like he's ready to strike at any moment. His eyes are rounded and taking everything in around him. Ice lives up to the road named given to him.

Carefully, I approach and hold out my hand to him. He glares at the gesture and recoils back. Not in fear of me but that he could harm me. Ice needs to see that he won't. He's not the animal he believes he is. Yes, he's deadly, but not deranged.

ICE

Dropping my hand, I turn on my heel and coax him along. "Come with me." In my bathroom, I turn on the shower for him. Old habits surface and I find a shopping bag and wait for Ice to join me in the bathroom. Stepping in, he looks confused this time. "Take your clothes off and jump in. You have blood on your hands and face." It's not much, but there are small splatters littered across his forehead he missed and slightly smeared across his hands.

He wants to tell me no, I can see it coming, but I don't allow it. Reaching the bottom of his shirt, I help to lift it up, initiating his movement. Then his pants. I start to unbuckle his belt while he kicks off his boots. A knife clatters on the tiled floor. By the looks of it, it's an average hunting knife made in the thousands, undetectable, not special. A toss-away weapon that is easy to discard.

Ice bends forward, picks up the knife from the floor, and steps into the shower. I watch him wash the blade clean of any traces of blood and set it on the edge of the tub. I gather his clothes and hat and place them into the plastic bag, knowing this is the last I'll ever see of these clothes.

It doesn't bother me. I love these men and have seen the worst of it. I believe in evil and no matter what side you're on, evil is everywhere. May as well side with the devil. Ice needs more in this life than darkness, and I want to give him what he gave me earlier, a new way to look at life. To believe in being different. He can love, he's just never allowed himself that.

Ice comes out of the bathroom with a towel wrapped around his waist. "Lay down." I pull the covers back and drop the robe that was around my naked body. Ice surprisingly shuts off the lights and slides in next to me. I don't waste time and curl into his side with my head on his bicep. My leg wraps up and over his. I take in a deep breath, memorizing his smell because nothing lasts forever. I'll have just two more nights with him and that is it.

"You bagged my clothes?" His deep throaty grumble vibrates through me.

"Yes. I may be a princess, Ice, but I was also a biker's Ol' Lady. We can be more than one thing at once, and in my experience, appearances are deceiving." I can't help but dig it in where I can for his earlier insult.

"Touché. Get some sleep."

And I do. I dream of a new life. One with possibilities of a man to settle down with.

It doesn't surprise me when I wake alone. Ice isn't a man to reciprocate intimacy. And it's fine with me. We agreed to experiment. All I wanted was to give him back what he gave me, peace. Turning on the T.V., I watch the news to see if anything major comes up, like a dead body. Thankfully, nothing does, and I sigh in relief.

It was as if it never even happened. The knife and clothes are gone from my room and from what I can tell, our suite altogether. In the main area, I find breakfast and coffee ready. Plopping into my seat across from Ice, I find Bella in his lap while he talks on the phone. It sounds like the norm of club business, who is doing what and when with their legal adventures. I tune it out and fill my cup with coffee, mixing in cream and sugar. Ben jumps into my lap while I eat.

ICE

I don't point out how cute Bella is with Ice because he will dump her on the floor and run. But it is incredibly cute how much she has taken to liking him. Ice is cold and withdrawn. He doesn't make any small talk and has retreated back to where we were the first day. I understand, you can only give what you can when you're ready or want to. He doesn't need or want a woman to take care of him. Who am I to judge? He is right about one thing—I am a princess. I *love* love, and I want to share my world with someone.

"You ready to go outside? C'mon, Bella, Ben, let's go." I leash the dogs and holler out, "Heading out."

Ice is off into his own world, being a grumpy miserable ass. A girl could use some sunshine and I plan on taking advantage of it. The dogs and I take a walk around the hotel and visit some shops to buy a few things to take home with me. I didn't realize until now how much I miss traveling. It feels as if I've awoken after years of being in a coma. The world feels, tastes, and looks completely new. My fingers trail over a delicate gold necklace with a small Las Vegas charm on it.

"That would look stunning on you," a man standing behind me comments.

"I haven't bought jewelry in a long time," I absently respond and turn around. My eyes pop at the gorgeous man in front of me in a stunning gray suit, dark hair and chiseled chin. "Maybe I will buy this one. Thank you." It is overpriced, but I want it. I want to remember this weekend every time I look at it.

"Are you free for dinner?"

My fingers drop away at the growl from behind me.

"No, she isn't free, ever." Tingles run up my spine and goosebumps cover my skin. The man smirks at Ice, not fazed by his possessive behavior.

He nods at me and winks before commenting, "I would do the same."

"Ice, is something wrong with you? You didn't want to come with me, and that man was only being nice." I forget about the necklace I wanted, the moment ruined, and I start my walk back to my room.

Ice stomps behind me. "Men aren't fucking nice, Harley."

"So? And women are bitches, yet here we are trying to match up bitches with assholes. Makes perfect sense to me."

Just like the first elevator ride we shared, it is heated. Is that what it was? Ice had a crush on me all along? I can't stop the chuckle in my throat from escaping and laughing out loud by myself.

"Something fuckin funny, Harley? I don't think you not coming back for over thirty minutes is funny, when I have to hunt you down."

"No, Ice, that's not funny. What is funny is you like me. You have for a while and I was too blind to see it."

"Thinking you're fuckable and likeable are two different things and I don't crush on women."

The elevator pops open and I turn to pat his cheek. "Okay, big guy." Reaching up, I kiss his cheek and saunter off to my room, shutting my door behind me to get ready for the show, which means a shower and a long afternoon of smiling.

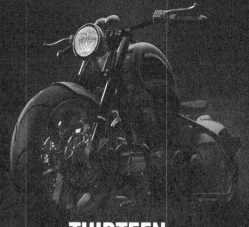

THIRTEEN

Ice

Harley is fucking wrong.

I didn't crush on her. I wanted her body, to take her flesh and use her for my own guilty pleasure. I'm torn between standing at her side and what I am here for, to keep an eyey on the men in the room. Vetting them for myself. If I had my way, I would drag her out of this gig, but I monitor the men walking around the showcase event for this year's motorcycles. Her pictures are plastered everywhere in the golden bikini from the shoot on cutouts and posters. I catch myself admiring the woman, who she was then and who she is now. The small wrinkles around her eyes, the widening of her hips.

My brothers from the Flagstaff show up for the event. Diesel hits my back. "You've been with this woman for how many days? From the looks of her brand on her back, she has an Ol' Man. Why isn't he here?"

"Had an old man. He passed in a freak accident a few years back." I don't explain much because I'm not giving him more information like I know he's wondering about.

past the awkward silence, I focus on the room, keeping tabs on her and the animals who circle around her. The building is packed with bikers of all kinds, from joyriders to fully pledged clubs.

Brian swarms around her, waiting for a break to catch her without me in arm's reach. He wants to get her alone to report a meeting time to the ATF agent, who I killed, to drill her with questions in a sad attempt to get the upper hand. They won't. Now that he's seen us together, two things have to happen, the first being, he will die by the end of the night. The how is going to piss off Harley. If I'm being honest, I like that it will.

The few hours she is required to sign autographs on the photos drags on. The grand finale of the event is the auction of this year's voted bike of the year. Harley stands up on stage, but something happens. Her face begins to fall. She is pulling away and crawling back into herself. With the spotlight on her, you would assume it's the stage, but it's more than that.

Harley

It hits me like a freight train that lost its brakes. The memories of us, Maddox and me, that fateful day, want to crush my heart into the floor. The weight of the sadness from missing him is so extreme, I want to fall to my knees. I want to die with him. The truth of it all, I wish I would have died in that accident too. The guilt of my feelings have been holding me back.

How could I not wish for it? I'm done. I want to run and leave and hide myself away from the shame. I take a step back, but I stall long enough that I don't leave. I hold myself steady and stare down the crowd, finally able to see the faces before me. Clearing my throat and then taking a deep breath, I relax my body. It's okay. I am who I am. I don't have to be the perfect princess at all times. I don't need to hide the truth or my pain.

The emcee holds the mic to me, hoping I snap out of it. Leaning forward, I take the mic. "It's been awhile," I start, and the crowd relaxes. "I can't tell you how much it means to me to be invited back to this event. This is where my life changed that day many years ago. Thank you for reminding me there is no going back but only forward. Nothing lasts forever, but the memories are ours to keep for eternity. Thanks again for the opportunity and joining us to present this year's best of show. Let the bidding begin!"

Handing back the mic, the crowd bursts out with hollers and calls as a volunteer biker drives the motorcycle onto the stage. I clap and my eyes fill with happiness and pride. I did this, I made it. The bike is parked, and like rapid-fire shots, the bike is auctioned while I do my very best to model and present the beautiful machine.

A very attractive man who I noticed was speaking with Ice purchases the bike and comes onstage to take pictures with me for the press. He holds my hand and gently rubs his thumb over my hand. "Pleasure to meet you."

"Thank you. I hope she brings you good luck. It did for me the last time I was here." He cocks his head to the side, amused there is a story behind my words. None that I want to share at this time. Pulling my hand away, I exit the stage, ready to go home, ready for my future. I'm surprised to find Brian at the dressing room doorway.

"You have time to join me for dinner tonight?"

The answer is no and it's on the tip of my tongue. I turn my body, looking for Ice as an excuse to get me out of his invite. The biker bitch plastered to his side down the hallway tells me he has plans and our fun is void. I need to eat, but mostly I do it out of spite. Fuck that asshole. "Sure, would you like to meet upstairs at the steakhouse?"

I give him back my full attention and plan on meeting in thirty minutes. In my dressing room, I think about wiping the makeup off but think better of it. Out of my bag, I pull a shimmery black dress I had planned to wear for Ice. I thought we could go out for drinks, this being our last night in the big city. Now, I am resigned to have this dinner and drinks alone at the bar. I change out of the bikini and I slide the dress over my body, sans bra or underwear. It's silk and the faintest line shines through.

Taking my small bag with me, I walk through the convention center floor. One last look, one last moment, and I thank God for all he has given me. I will cherish this experience as one of the best in my life, coming full circle, a new life and rebirth. A chance to start over.

A chill runs down my spine. Anxiety crawls at my throat, forcing me to turn my head. The draw is powerful through the crowd, but those piercing light gray/blue eyes mesmerize me, so hard and cold, they arrest me, freezing me to the spot at which I stand. I wish he were different, but he's not. It's better to break free now.

I turn my back on Ice. I ignore the what-if's and believe if he were to be mine, he would be. I will never fight for a man to love me, and he has made it clear he doesn't do love. With every step, the chains he has around my thoughts start to untwine. Every step is a little bit clearer until I push him away all together. At the concierge's desk, I ask him to hold my bag, take out my wallet, and begin the long journey to the restaurant.

A warm hand slides across my lower back and I freeze at the crushing grip at my hip. Only one man has ever commanded me to listen without words. Ice. "Where do you think you are going?" His voice has changed to a melodic threat.

My body leans into his and soaks up his strength and brutality. "To dinner," I say simply.

"We had a deal."

"We did. You broke it when another woman touched you. I promised to be yours. If I wasn't clear, it went both ways. I don't share, ever, Ice. Deal is off." Leaning up on my toes, I place a light kiss on his jaw, meant to tell him goodbye.

Ice traps me to him with his iron hold, his arms encasing me as his prisoner. "You forget, sexy, this body is mine until I let it go." An involuntary shiver takes over my skin at the chilling threat begging me to bow to him. My hands run over his chest and cut. I am a slave to his strength and power.

"Ice," I pause, his name tasting like a bad word on my lips, "I'll beg for your affection and deliver my submission only when you give me yours."

"I don't submit for anyone."

"No, Ice, your affection, your devotion." His grip tightens before he lets me go and I have my answer as suspected.

I know I need a man who will be mine as much as I am his. He waits for me to fight, to push him into a corner, to choose, but I will not. "We still need to eat. Let's go."

It's not what he was expecting from me. He believes me to be some princess and high maintenance woman. Ice has just scratched the surface. He leads the way to where I am supposed to be going. His control and dominance is a comforting show. Like he told me just days ago, I will not settle, and I need more, so much more. I know what love is, and it doesn't have to be exactly the same as before, but the passion for each other's happiness is a boundary I won't sacrifice.

FOURTEEN

Ice

Her nipples are hard as rocks under the silk covering them. I saw the look of disappointment cross her face when she saw Lexi hanging off me. She is an old flame I haven't been with in years. It was necessary for her to take whatever Brian offered for the next phase in my plan to work. As soon as she walked out in that dress, every man's head turned. Many started in her direction, until I stopped them. No one was going to touch the skin on her body. Harley is mine and I am far from done with her. My obsession startled me, but she is a siren calling to me.

The look on Brian's face when I enter the restaurant is priceless. It goes from excited to an ashen pale color. I drained his hopes and dreams. He doesn't know he has already lost and soon he will die. If I go through with what I am about to, to protect both of us, I may sacrifice any chance of ever being near her again. I've never considered a reaction of this magnitude. Never cared what a woman would think of me and had no need to care. The circumstance is so foreign that it is impossible to back out. I know only one thing—to kill and get the job done.

The waiter comes as soon as we sit and I order champagne to congratulate Harley on her success. She eyes me wearingly, knowing this is a show. Brian holds up his glass and compliments her beauty. Gracefully, she thanks him, and even I can even tell she is bored. There is no bite for bold sexiness. She needs raw, unfiltered appeal. My hand slides over her thigh. The silk transmits heat between us. She chokes on her drink before refilling her glass.

Harley still belongs to me and will give me what I want by the end of the night. "Why don't we meet up at the new nightclub that opened a few blocks from here? It's our last night."

"I don't see why not," Brian agrees. The fool thinks he has me where he wants me. The more alcohol we drink, the more he is convinced of it. What he doesn't notice is how much water I have drank in between. He feels like a man with how many drinks he's put down.

Harley knows we have begun a game and watches me closely, eating the last few bites of her dinner. "I would love to, but don't we need to get up early?"

"No, we aren't leaving early. Let me take you out." She nods and continues finishing her meal. "Brian, why don't you meet us there? We will head over now, after I make a few calls."

He agrees and excuses himself, I'm sure to go call his ATF agent to meet us there. "What are you doing?" she hisses into my ear. My hand, still on her leg, squeezes. "Drink and enjoy your night. I have work to do and I need you to not worry about the rest." My words are biting, but she huffs and downs the last drop.

ICE

"Be careful what you ask for, Ice." It seems my sexy woman has claws and my dick gets hard at her, like a dog wanting meat. It makes me want to pull up her dress and fuck her from behind to show her who is the boss. She bites her bottom lip to egg me on, excitement flashing across her face. Something akin to pride weaseles in. I wouldn't call it love, but Harley is mine. No man will have what she has to offer. Ever. Since she wants it, why wouldn't I give her what we both crave?

This game between us has grown. It all started with the devastation inside such a beautiful creature. She lured me in. Haunted my dreams with her desperation to be free of the pain. I wanted to kill her then, strangle her with my bare hands and give her the ultimate pleasure, peace. I woke up hard countless times after dreaming of her. Crying with me strangling her. Me being her savior. Harley has haunted me for years, a morbid fascination I never let go of. She doesn't know, but she was always mine. Harley wormed her way inside me even further with her quirks and penetrated the cold barrier around my heart.

Together, we take a taxi and I lead her around to the back service entrance. Harley plays the part of the super-model and struts up the back ramp like there was a red carpet rolled out for her. Maximus, the head of security, takes my cut and hands me a black button up shirt. Harley wanders over to a cook in the back and he is already giving her dessert samples. She moans and asks for more. Much to his amusement, he gives her more. Fuck, I want to fuck the shit out of her, and those sounds are going to distract me from my job. In the very least, postpone it.

With the shirt haphazardly buttoned up, I yank her

and her tits away from the chef and lead her out to the floor where we wait. "You wanted a night out, Ice, here it comes." She orders us a set of shots at the bar. "Eight hours left. Whatever happens, happens." She holds up her drink and clinks it to mine.

I take the shot and then order a couple of waters while she takes another shot. The base thumps and the music pulsates around us. The crowd is a hot, sweaty mix of lust and energy intoxicating the young. What they fail to see are the predators in their mix. Harley rubs her body against mine, her hips swaying back and forth across my dick. She reaches up, her nails scratch across my jawline.

She needs me to make her come undone, the way only I can. To feel the tangible existence of the desire between us, an imaginary connection linking me to her. The draw is undeniable. Protectively, I lay a hand on her lower back. She takes from me, my strength and power and lays her trust in me. Her words snap together from earlier.

"Show me your affection and devotion, and I'll give you my submission."

She has stolen parts of me I was never willing to give or saw coming. She is the predator. All the same, I let it ride. For one night, I go all in at what it means to give her true desires. For one night, I claim her as mine. Her existence belongs to only me.

Brian shows not long after and I order him enough drinks to put down a horse as the night wears on. He starts to sweat and the drugs I dropped into his drink bring his blood pressure to a dangerous high. He starts to pant and pulls at his shirt collar before announcing that he needs to go outside.

As low as I can, I yell over the music, "Sit at the bar, don't move, and don't talk to anyone." She gives me a nod. Harley's eyes glisten with anticipation in the lights from above. My fingers brush her ass as I walk past, a reminder to listen and that I'm coming back for her.

I lead him stumbling through the dance floor and out the back doors into the alleyway behind the nightclub. Not one employee flinched at the sight. They keep their heads down, as they are paid to. We barely reach the back doors when he begins to vomit and convulse from the drugs. Brian's hands reach for me to save him, not knowing I am the one who killed him. He played in a game he should have never got involved in. I gave him mercy when it could have been so much worse.

While I wait for the drugs to take hold and pull him under, I pull out my phone, making a call to a cop on payroll. "He's done." He'll be here when the call goes out of a cold, dead body in the back. The paid cop will make sure to be here first and fix the paperwork. A waitress who works for the club walks out of the shadows. She'll call it in, say saw him come out alone and fall to the ground, his body twitching and then nothing.

Nodding at her, I walk back into the nightclub. My feet falter when I see Harley's face. She knows she will never see Brian again and not to ask the details of why.

FIFTEEN

Harley

A cold chill stops my heart. I witnessed a murder. Well, I didn't see him die, but I know Ice killed him, and right then, I was a pawn in his game this whole time. I'm too drunk to remember any details of their interactions to figure out why Brian would be a threat. I know the club did things to protect us, but I haven't been a witness to it.

Quickly, he makes his way through the crowd and his fingers dig into my jaw. Painfully, they capture my full attention in my intoxicated condition. Ice's cold stare holds mine and I beg him to make this alright. "It had to be done, to protect you."

I believe him.

Why it would makes no sense to me. I don't really know Ice to trust him like this, but I do. He senses my unspoken questions instantly. "Don't worry, Harley, and don't ask questions." His teeth run along my neck. I reach for him and grip his shirt, my body relaxing into him. Ice palms my ass and grinds his dick against my stomach. "I need to feel that you are mine. Will you submit to me now?" His breath feathers across my skin. Ice's words are a feral growl.

There is no doubt in my mind because my body would betray me even if I wanted to say no. Ice leads me through the drunken crowd to the back VIP area and private restrooms. He is forceful in his pursuit, making it hard for me to keep up in my heels. But he never lets go, holding my hand, not permitting me to fall behind. We barrel into the empty bathroom stall. The door ricochets off the stall wall. His mouth is on my mine in a kiss he has never delivered before. He takes my lips and tongue. I dare to believe he gives me the intimacy I've craved and missed. He may not say the words, but Ice shows me his devotion, even if it is just for now. I crave it like I need my next breath.

I give him everything back. With every thrust of my tongue, we fuck each other's mouths until it's not enough. Ice tugs and pulls my dress up around my hips. He groans when he sees my exposed pussy with no underwear. "You were made to fuck, Harley."

My dress is pulled down from my shoulders next, the material pooling at my waist. His mouth sucks at my nipples while he caresses my clit with his fingers, bringing me to the edge. "Fuck me, Ice. Own me. Make me come for you." My skin tingles and electricity shoots through my spine.

He growls and spins me around, pinning me to the door with his weight. The sound of his zipper ignites my desire to feel him rocking his steel length between my legs. I arch my back and pop my ass out, widening my legs, waiting for his entrance.

The condom wrapper hits the floor. The head of

his dick nudges at my entrance before he powers inside. Together, we groan and fuck like the dirty porn stars we have become. It's all a haze of lust and liquor from that point on.

I fucked Ice up against the bathroom stall. My mind starts to wake and the memories start to surface slowly. He wanted me, needed me, and I gave him everything. My soul was eaten by him in one bite. I loved every minute of his desire. He pulled my dress up and over my ass, groaning at my bare pussy on display for his use. I wanted him to have me and he took it. He slid inside and took more than I ever thought a man could ever again. Ice corrupted what was left of my heart and took it as a prisoner.

We ran out of there, the club being too much for us. After a long day, I needed peace to gather my thoughts. Inside of the taxi, I whisper, "Ice, I'm worried. What if when we are apart, they come after me?" Who, I don't know, but the reality is a choking fear—I will be alone and he will be miles away when we go home.

"I'll make sure they can never question you," he rasps back into my ear. Ice suddenly directs the driver to stop. Screeching to a halt, he does as ordered. I follow Ice out of the car to the sidewalk and look up at the sign of the building while he asks the taxi driver to wait. "Little Chapel of Love." I choke on the words, gasping and whipping around to him. The heart in my chest pounds like I just ran a marathon.

"Trust me," he orders.

ICE

For the third time tonight, I want to see this wild thing through.

I want Ice.

I said "I do" in a black dress.

I married a cold-hearted killer who brought me back to life.

Fear overrides my actions. My heart thumps through my veins like a thunderbolt. I need to get out of here. I had sex and married the man who made my darkest fantasies come true last night. The animalistic look on his face and his demands made me putty in his hands. I wanted it. I loved every minute of it. What does that make me? Hungry for Ice. If I stay, the further I will fall in love with him.

Groaning, I roll over and bump into a naked chest. Ice lays with his arms out and on his back. My mind is a fuzzy mess with how much alcohol I drank. I run through the events of the entire day, but nothing makes any sense and I am so confused. Why did he kill Brian? Did he marry me to keep me quiet, and I complied like a puppet?

Sitting up, the sheet falls around my bare body. Guilt, shame, and, most of all, fear wash over me. Ice will leave me one day.

For the first time in my life, I have the urge to run and hide. Dodge the reckless choices I've made, ones I want to keep to myself. My very own secret that belongs just to me. I loved every single second of it, even if he did it to save his own ass.

85

SIXTEEN

Ice

My morning wood is the first thing I notice as I start to wake up. Next, is the taste of the leftover whiskey in my mouth. For a second, I believe I am back at my clubhouse in Elko. The scenario is familiar to what is usually normal. Except, I am not in Elko.

There is nothing normal about the empty halo of quietness in this room. I sit straight up in bed and look around for any signs of Harley. Shit, I slept in, passed out drunk. The last thing I remember...

Harley is breathtaking in the black dress caressing every curve of her body. Her eyes twinkle with mischief. I can't look away from her angelic face. She repeats the words from the overweight Elvis impersonator who is our wedding officiant. Harley said yes, that she would be my wife.

She was scared and I didn't know how to comfort her, to find the right words. Even now, I only did this for my own selfish reasons. Harley will never be able to testify against me as long as we stay married. It was part of my plan. Keep her

*tethered to me any way possible. The dick in me also didn't
want her to leave here with her newfound freedom and screw
the next guy who piqued her interest. I had no intention of
taking her home either. How this was going to work, I wasn't
sure, but the first reason seemed like the best choice.*

*I could keep her tied to me for as long as I wanted. Drive
into Reno and fuck my wife, convincing her that keeping our
marriage a secret is smart. That way, the ATF agents don't
keep snooping around her. I've thought of a million ways to
manipulate this. All of them are selfish and all of them may end
up with a bullet in my skull.*

*Elvis asks me to take her to be my wife in sickness and
health till death do us part.*

*"Until death do us part." I mean every fucking word.
Harley may have been scared of the agents coming for her, but
I was scared to lose her. This is what I am, a man willing to
win at all costs and take what he wants for as long as he wants.
Harley is never leaving me.*

*After our wedding, I bought whiskey, laid my wife out on
the bed, and fucked her with no condom. Drunk and carefree,
I gave her pieces of me she wouldn't understand. I made love to
her. I claimed her as my own.*

I would panic, except without moving, I can see her
bags are gone. Her room is empty, and she ran at the
first chance she got. Anger explodes through my veins.
Throwing the covers off, I stomp my naked ass across the
suite and check my stuff. The keys to the SUV are gone.
Harley left me stranded in Las Vegas and I would bet my
last dollar she is halfway home by now.

Pulling on a pair of shorts, I stomp back over to her

room, locate my phone, and call River. He picks up quickly, "Are you heading back now? Late start. Did you two go to an after party?" He jokes, but it would be an accurate account of what happened.

"I'm in some trouble," I inform him before I collapse onto a chair. "I took care of the rat and an ATF agent. Harley knows about the rat, so I married her last night."

All I hear is choking and spitting on the other end of the line. "Are you fucking with me right now? Where is she?"

"Harley took off while I was passed out drunk. I'm assuming she's halfway to Reno by now. I don't know what time she ran out of here. She's gone and so is the car we drove down in."

The manic laughter fills the line and my irritation grows. "Your bride, the first woman you ever got yourself hitched to, ditched you the first chance she got."

"That's the least of my problems at the moment, asshole. I need you to get me back to Reno. Either find the next flight out of here or a car, whatever is fastest, and get it done. I'm going to have a bullet in my head by the time I catch up to her. They aren't going to be too happy she drove across Nevada alone."

"That's if she doesn't tell before she gets back. How are they going to react to all this? Her eloping with you drunk?"

"It's not going to go over well. Axl will be pissed. There is a code. He's going to feel like I betrayed him and his brothers will back him."

"There is only one thing," River contemplates. "If she covers for you, it may stay under the radar. I'll get you out of there, stay by your phone."

He hangs up and his words spin around in my mind. That's a big if, and I have never seen in my lifetime when a woman covered for me. She belongs to their club, and in the light of day, she will start to connect the dots of why I was here and how the clubs manipulated her trip to do club business. How she takes what we did, especially me, is a wild card.

SEVENTEEN

Harley

I had to stop multiple times and buy energy drinks for the long eight-hour drive home. The entire ride, my body was wired with anxiety that I would, for one, be hauled off to a federal prison for witnessing what I did and doing nothing to stop it.

The second thing I couldn't let go was my guilt for marrying another man. I knew I was ready to start a slow relationship, but to be married? I willingly jumped into this mess headfirst. So much for taking it slow and step-by-step. I didn't consider a second marriage as a possibility in my life. I assumed I would have a long-term boyfriend, one where we could live together.

My mind swims in a sea of doubt. Why would my son be okay with me coming down here with another club? Yes, they know Ice, but there are other men who could have gone on this trip. Then Brian's face pops into my mind. I feel sick to my stomach. He seemed to me to be a nice guy. Eager to get to know me, but what is the crime in that?

I am too amped up to make any sense of it all, so I

make a call to one person who I know can help me. "Kat, I need you to meet me at my house in two hours, alone."

Kat is married to the Battle Born Road Captain, and also has an extensive background of let's say getting away with hiding dead bodies and information you don't want revealed.

"Are you safe? Where are you?" Both of those questions fall out of her mouth in rapid succession.

"Yes, I am safe. I'm driving home alone. I'll meet you at my house."

"Turn off your phone, and only turn it back on in an emergency." She hangs up on her end. That really didn't help ease my fears at all. In fact, she made me feel even more paranoid. I do as she instructed and turn off my phone before tossing it back in my bag.

The last couple of hours crawl by at a snail's pace. I count every mile marker. My only saving grace is that Bella and Ben are sitting here with me. At least I am not alone, it helps. I've never been so happy to see the city in the horizons and I step on the gas.

Weaving through the city streets, I inch a little closer to my home. The small house never looked so good. I pull into the driveway and my blood pressure skyrockets seeing Tank waiting. Pulling in, he is shaking his head at me.

I park and jump out, wanting to kiss the ground that I made it home. Instead, I face off with Tank and wonder if he's told my son what is going on. Tank's eyebrow raises and his arms cross his chest before he starts in, "I don't know what trouble you managed to get yourself into, and I will find out more later. Kat has your back, whatever you need. You shouldn't have run off alone, ever. Go inside. As far as I know, you made it home safe." His face relaxes and the large grin lets me know his rant is over. "What was I supposed to do, ask you a million questions? I just drove the SUV from your house then back as asked."

Tank, Kat's Ol' Man, wraps me in a big hug. "Whatever has you running, we will take care of it." For the first time in hours, I finally truly exhale and let go. The dogs jump around at my feet, excited to be home as much as I am. I walk inside to find Kat waiting inside the living room. I don't ask how she got in, she does what she wants.

"I would offer you a coffee, but it looks as if you made yourself at home already."

Kat smirks with a drink already in hand. The dogs excitedly run around my feet before they beeline for the back doggy door. "Sit down, start at the beginning, and tell me all the details."

Exhausted, I fall to the couch, enjoying the comfort of being home. I tell her everything from start to finish, leaving out the very intimate details, but she understands just how serious the relationship got.

Kat taps her chin and sits in silence while the information runs through her mind. "There obviously is much more missing on his side of the story, like you think. Let's separate the facts from the feelings first. The guys purposely asked Ice to take you for a good reason. We both know they wouldn't make a decision like that lightly." She takes a sip of her drink and looks me dead in the eye. "They did use this as an opportunity to settle something. Question is, do you want to know why?"

"I don't need to know. Ice went to settle business. I've never been used as a cover and I now question it all. How my son and the club I've been part of took this opportunity. I'm so mad, it feels like they took something from me, something that belonged to me."

"I can see why it would look that way. I also think you're pissed and giving them too much of your anger. They knew something beforehand. Ice was there for a reason. You're pissed because you fucked Ice and loved it and married his dick. Why even be mad at that? It was a good weekend regardless, right? Get out of your head. Life isn't black and white. It's messy as hell. We both know that. Make the best of it, let the rest go."

I'm ready to say the words out loud, that it was a rush like none other I have felt before. It was a drug that scared me. Would I become addicted to it? I felt guilt and shame for it. The thrill to kill was an aphrodisiac I've never experienced. Ice is a cold-hearted killer. One I felt for a night belonged to me. It made me feel like a queen. By the morning, I felt like a fool and ran for the car the first chance I got. I ran because rejection would have ruined it.

"I know you have a lot on your mind. Don't be hard on yourself. You're not perfect, Harley. Just be you, and fuck everyone else. Simple as that. And if they sent Ice with you, and something happened to that man while you were there, that is why Ice was there. My advice is let the details go. It's not your business anyway and you don't want to play in their playground."

"What if the cops come questioning me for answers?" Now that is a reality I didn't want to think of or deal with. I don't want to call Axl and tell him. He'll flip out and ask questions I know he won't want answers to.

"They aren't. You married him, remember? Stop focusing on the shit you don't need to be focusing on. Do you know how many people saw him alive before he died? Sounds to me like another partier took a night too far in Sin City. Ice wouldn't put you in a position. Not that kind, anyway." She smirks a wicked gleam.

"Then why did he marry me?" We were caught up in what happened, but still, I feel like I'm missing something.

Kat laughs long and hard. "He wanted you. Ice took advantage of you and your vulnerabilities to tie you to him. Ice does nothing but take care of himself first. His motive was selfish. You came back married to the coldest, most calculating son-of-a-bitch I know this side of the border. He didn't accidentally say *I do*. He was in control since he first made you put on the seatbelt. Honey, he's a Dom and five steps ahead of you, until now."

"What does that mean?"

"He didn't release you on his terms, you walked out on him. Tell me, how do you think he will react to the fact you abandoned him?"

Cold runs through my body. What will he do? A shiver runs up my spine. "I thought he was using me, that he would dump me."

"I wouldn't be so sure on that one." She pats my leg. "Stop freaking out, Harley. You lived a weekend most wouldn't experience. Don't feel guilty for living. Enjoy the ride. My advice, call Ice and tell him where you are and make-up, so you don't get his ass in trouble."

I never thought he would get into trouble for me running out on him. But now that she said it, would Axl and the Battle Born be pissed off for what happened between us? I'm betting he will find a way to bury what we did and no one will know. I'm running with *"What happens in Vegas, stays in Vegas."*

EIGHTEEN

Ice

"**F**uck this shit."

I know River is working on getting me out of here. The longer I sit and wait, the more pissed off I get. I'm an impatient motherfucker and the longer I am here, my temper gets hotter by the second. Harley left me here. Abandoned me to find my own way back. Left without so much as *"hey, it was nice fucking you while it lasted."* Bitches run off after they get what they want.

I jammed my small duffle bag with my belongings and swing that shit over my back. Checking my pockets, I pat my sides down to check and get the hell out of this hotel. They have my card on file, and we were checking out today anyway. I'm about to turn right and head out of the lobby when a piece of jewelry catches my eye.

The gold shines in the case. It's the same necklace Harley wanted to buy for herself just a day or so ago. It calls to me to buy it. I can't place my finger on the why, and I don't take the time to analyze it, but my gut tells me to take it with me. I pull open the case and hold the delicate gold chain in my fingers. It's fine and beautiful. Walking over to the register, I pay for the token of truth, a good luck charm. I'll have the last word. If nothing else, I'll use it to pay Harley back for skipping out on me. I'll send it to her as a reminder that you can run from your choices, but you can't hide.

I pluck a card from the stand and add it to the purchase. "She is going to love this," the salesgirl comments, gently wraps the necklace in tissue paper, and folds it together in a box. With skilled hands, she ties a ribbon and passes them both over. "Is she your wife?" she questions.

"No, she's a bitch who left me. She's not walking away with the last word." I pin her with a fierce stare. "Do yourself a favor, Tiffany, stay off your back."

Her mouth drops open and wants to argue both comments. I don't care if her name is Tiffany or not, they are all the same and the comment about not being a slut is a favor. Maybe she'll hate me enough to stay away from assholes like me.

Snatching the bag from her, I storm out of the shop and hit the road. Flagging down a taxi, I ask him to take me to a car rental place and hand him a twenty, saying, "Hurry the hell up and I got another one for you." The wheels squeal as we peel out and horns blare at us.

The cab driver asks me no questions and I prefer it that way. Just as I said, I passed him another twenty and his fare before I get out. I rent the fastest car they have, a Dodge Charger, and hit the road. I call River to let him know I'm on my way. He's tracked Harley's phone and, as I thought, she is almost to Tonopah.

Zipping through traffic, I'm on the chase to hunt her

down for one purpose, to let her know that we are over. "Let the highway patrol know I'm coming through and my plate number." With that, I hang up the phone and hit the gas, weaving through traffic.

The distance across the desert does nothing to calm down the rage inside. If anything, it makes it worse. The sand and brush is miles and miles of deserted hot land. I'm pissed that she left alone. If something happened to her, it would be my fault. If her car broke down and highway thieves found her alone, she couldn't defend herself. Hundreds of people go missing on these empty highways. A good percentage is because we want them gone, but that other percentage is unknown. Even the ATF could pick her up.

My mind starts to spin of other possibilities. Could Harley be working with them, sharing intel to save her own ass? Those assholes would tell her she would be saving her son and she wouldn't even know that it was all bullshit. My hand slams on the steering wheel and I turn up the heavy metal on the stereo.

Heat radiates up my back from the leather seats and I turn up the air. Anything could happen to her. I stay focused on one thing—making sure she is safe. Then I'm leaving for good. She will never see my face again.

My phone rings about an hour later and I answer River. "Harley's phone went off just outside of Tonopah, Grim's territory. He said they saw her driving through and are tailing her home. Rest easy, brother, she is okay."

"Thanks, brother. Apparently, she thinks that will stop us from finding her. I have one thing to drop off, then I'm getting my bike and I'm heading home. Be there by dark."

The last few hours take the longest. The closer I get to Reno, I slow down. I'm about three hours behind Harley, so I don't really know what to expect when I roll into her neighborhood. I pull my handgun out from the bag and tuck it into my pants after I park on the curb. It appears quiet, but that can also mean a trap.

I've never been afraid and I'm not starting to be a chicken shit today. Slamming the car door shut, two heads pop up from the couch. One I make out to be Harley and the other is Kat. I've worked with her before and know she can be deadly in her own right, but she wouldn't set herself up to be seen if she wanted me dead.

I take out the box and card I bought before I left, and with long purposeful strides, I barge into Harley's house. With a blaze in my heart, I toss the box and card at her chest. Harley's mouth hits the floor. This is the last time she will see my face and fury. After today, never again.

Kat stands and matches my stature, ready to fight. "No one knows what happened and we are going to keep it that way."

I hold her glare and look for any lies. When I can't find any, I nod, "I need to dump the car and get my bike."

"I'll take you and drop you off." Tossing Kat the keys, she follows me out to the rental and slides into the driver's seat. "I'll return the car today too."

I grunt in response. Kat will do what she says, because of all the people I have met, she's kept the biggest secrets. "Keep this between us. I'll clean it up." Meaning I will divorce and erase what happened between Harley and I.

"I would do it for you, but also plausible deniability and all that." Kat has a killer smile and takes a left hand turn in the opposite direction of the clubhouse. She picks up on my discomfort and clarifies the change in route. "The SUV is parked at my house. Take it to the clubhouse, no one will know."

"Tank?"

"He knows, but he cares for Harley. He'll keep it quiet. You were Battle Born once, Ice, still a brother, still have loyalty. And why wouldn't we? You've been helping to keep my dead husband buried along with all of our secrets, keeping ATF guessing and all of us out of prison."

My eyebrows raise because Tank is the polar opposite of Kat, his Ol' Lady. He loves to spread the drama for entertainment.

"Don't worry. He saw the look on Harley's face. He won't hurt her." Meaning, he won't gossip about her personal shit for kicks.

There is one thing about secrets, they are only kept if the ones who know them are dead. It likely will come out and I'll be ready.

NINETEEN

Harley

I read the card over and over. "Everything will be erased and forgotten within twenty-four hours. Keep your mouth shut. P.S., I got you a token to remember what it was like to have me fuck you like you didn't deserve."

My hands shake holding the card scrolled by his hand, angry and slashed across the Thank You, or more like Fuck You, card. I'm stuck on the words and I am afraid to see what is inside the decorated giftbox. Pain lances my heart, beautifully raw. Where did we go wrong? We are the definition of fire and ice. He is a terrifying man, one who thinks I betrayed him. We were never going to last, so why be so angry with me?

Did I betray him though? I was terrified of who I was, not him. I ran from myself and gave into the weakness of my fear. I ran before he could hurt me, so I did it first. I really messed up. My hands unwind the ribbon and I slowly lift the lid on the giftbox. Inside is the beautiful gold chain with a charm. I remember that day and I wanted to buy the jewelry for myself to remember who I have become, a token for me. What this weekend was about, me being brave enough to be different. No one else. For him to throw this in my face is so insulting. I would throw it into the trash, but I'm pissed.

Ice has another thing coming if he thinks I will cower to him and his stubborn temperamental ways. Fuck him. I take the card and light it on fire in the metal pan in the backyard. Charging inside the house, I find a large envelope and toss the necklace with the box inside. I don't bother wrapping the ribbon, I just toss that inside too. I took the envelope the card came in outside and scraped the burned and charred card back inside. Licking the glue, I press it shut. Inside in my purse, I find a bright red lipstick and seal it with a kiss.

I tape up my package and drive to the nearest FedEx and overnight that goodbye back to Ice. I will get the last word. I'm nobody's puppet.

TWENTY

Ice

My bad day turned worse when River sent me a text that heat has been coming down on the stable he runs for the club. One of his top-earning girls has gone missing. Most of these girls fly in from all over the country and world to work. They stay for the week and then return home to their families. You would never know that a woman attending your local PTA is a high-paid escort. Her not showing up to work means we both are taking a hit in income. Chloe nets a million a year and was published in the newspapers as the highest-paid escort of the year. She also has two kids at home. We need to find out why she hasn't checked in and STAT.

I'm in no mood to be messed with when I storm into the clubhouse and am greeted by my brothers. Storm, Easy, Chains, and River meet me at the table along with our brothers. Sliding into my seat, I hit the gavel and the door is locked. "What do we know and for how long?"

River, my VP, takes a breath. "Chloe was to check in yesterday. Storm called to see if she missed her flight and he hasn't heard from her. I located her sister's phone number and she hasn't answered either. Chloe has an appointment with a high-paying regular tomorrow. He's flying in to see her. Should I call him?"

Running two hands over my head and a week's worth of whiskers, I make a call I don't want to make. Chloe could practically keep the lights on with just her income. "Cancel the week. Whatever is going on, we don't want it to get out. Let them know she had a personal emergency and we will cover any expenses as needed."

River deflates back as the rest do. I press on. Regardless, we have work to do. "We also need to consider she may not be coming back. Storm, I need you to start showcasing up and coming talent and get a positive buzz feed going. Toss Tina into the pool."

For a moment, the room is silent. Tossing her in the stable of girls means she's free game to all of them. If Tina gives us any issues, she'll get banned. I do it to protect myself. I do it because Harley is stuck in my head, and until I can clean up my mess, I'm not touching another woman. My hands clench at the idea of choking Harley to death. I may have had my hand in the events, but it doesn't mean I don't want to teach her a lesson either.

"Good idea, Prez. I'll get on it," Storm confirms.

I'm given the rundown of all the business updates since I last spoke with River. Nothing out of the ordinary for them. For me, I'm in a fucked-up spot. Slamming down the gavel, the room clears out. River hovers over me and it just adds to my frustration. "What?" I snap.

"What's got you so fucking twisted, Prez?"

My jaw tenses and I grind my teeth. Not wanting to

go down this road, it is better that he knows. "I hooked up with Harley." It's pissing me off. My chest is tight and I can't get the right words out. Everything feels wrong and foreign. I've never been in this place in my life. All it does is make me feel murderous.

His eyebrows raise surprised but not really getting the whole picture. "People hook up all the time. Of which, we already went over…"

"It's Harley. Mad Max's Ol' Lady." I try to explain, more so for myself than him. "She is property of the Battle Born. At least that is the way Axl, her son, is going to see it. Especially when he finds out I married her last night and she went home alone. It's not going to be good for business. Fuck, I did what I always said I wouldn't. This could be a problem for the club."

River's eyes bug out. "Is that why you kicked Tina to the curb? Then hammered it home by putting her to work in the brothel?"

"I am a fucked-up asshole, but I do have boundaries. I won't fuck around if I'm married and that is why I need it covered. Get it annulled and erased, like it never happened."

He shakes his head, disbelieving what I just said. "How did this happen between you two? I thought it was a job, not a social engagement, or I would have tagged along. You could bring her here to talk. Battle Born may be okay with it, if you two can work things out before they find out."

"It wasn't supposed to happen. Fuck, I'm not talking about it. Just make sure it is covered and quiet." My gut twists with those words. My club has always been number

one. Why does this bug me so much then? I was going to get my fill and move on as I usually do. But it's Harley, the woman who has haunted me with those green eyes.

River reluctantly agrees and leaves me alone with my thoughts. I sit in this big empty room and have never felt so pissed off at my own actions than I do now. For years, I've chosen this life. Years and hundreds of women I can't even remember anymore. Never would I settle down. My old man rode with the Royal Bastards until he died years back from liver failure. I was raised in the MC life. I've only ever known women to be club whores and to treat them like one.

I lost my virginity to one when I was fourteen. Granted, I aged quickly living just with my old man. Seen shit no kid ever should. She was younger, probably barely eighteen, my dad passed her a hundred and she was more than willing to get me off. After a while, she was gone. He taught me that once they start to mean anything, you turn them loose, move on. I've been doing that ever since.

He didn't talk much, if ever, about my mother. She probably was some hanger-on. Never gave much thought about her and never cared. I still don't. But I do wonder why I did what I did with Harley. I gave her more than I have anyone. It's time to let her go.

"Prez!" Storm stomps down the hallway. "FedEx sent a package." We all cringe at what could be in the box. We have all seen in the movies where a body part is sent as a message. Well, we've lived that scene more than once.

"Shit." He slides the box across the desk and I slowly start to rip the tab open. We both are thinking the same thing—is some part of Chloe in this box? Inside, there is another large envelope and the return address is a name I wasn't expecting to see in a million years. 'Your ex-wife' is written in bold block letters. "It's nothing. Give me a moment."

Storm grumbles something about nothing doesn't usually comes delivered to your door via FedEx. There is no way I will let him see what could possibly be inside. Ripping the package open, I find the box with the necklace and then the card.

On the back of the envelope is an imprint of those fucking lips in bright red lipstick. I pop it open to find the charred remains of our marriage. Game over. If two people were ever divorced on their own terms, Harley and I found an original way to do it.

As much as I want to be pissed off, I'm not. I fucking miss the bitch. Miss her laughs, smiles, and attitude. Any other person, it would have been a war, but with her, it's a game. Foreplay to the main event. I consider calling River back in here to tell him not to do anything at all. My pride stops me from doing it. It's better this way, even if my gut tells me I'm dead wrong. I ignored it for the first time in my life.

TWENTY-ONE

Harley

The week crawls by painfully slow. Ice has been on my mind and in my dreams. There, he does things to my body that make me wake up panting and frustrated. During the day, I miss his crabby personality. It's better this way, to walk away before it went too far.

I try to smile through the questions about my trip to Las Vegas. I wasn't made to hide secrets. I'm transparent with the world. It eats me alive that I gave myself to someone, a piece of me, and it was carelessly tossed aside. I am the girl who lived a fairytale, and now I am realizing those don't really exist. I was young and naive before, early in my life, but events have changed who I am. They all have shaped me into the woman I am now. I will never be the same Harley from before again. I learned that much. She died too and I didn't expect to see that coming.

I may not believe in fairytales anymore, but I found out I am not a one-night stand, temporary fill-in. Commitment is still huge to me. It's just the type of person I am. Kudos to those who have that capability to only need a lover for the night.

"I need a full-time boyfriend." I announced it unexpectedly at our lunch. The girls, Dana, Jenn, Vegas, and Kat, are here at the Prez's home. All eyeballs pop open and I continue to elaborate about the trip, how being there made me realize how lonely I was and am ready to move on. I don't give them details of how I came to that conclusion, but I share enough.

I kept them away as long as I could and said I caught the flu while down there. What I caught was feelings and I wasn't about to admit any of that. Dana demanded we meet for the details today and I gave in. "It was good for me to go down there and push myself to figure out who I am now. That's been the missing piece. I changed over the years and I found her. I'm darker and more cynical about life. You could say I see the world at face value, no more bullshit. Life is not a fairytale."

Several heads nod and Dana, my daughter-in-law, comments, "It's okay that you did think that. Nothing's wrong with that. What happened down there that brought all this up?"

Holding my drink, I think about her question. Ice, and his monster ego and dick, was a game changer. He didn't give me any special treatment. He shot it straight, and I needed the tough love to break through the cycle I hadn't seen before. "I just want to live again. The key was finding the desire inside, finding out who I am. I was just stuck, and it was like a lightning bolt struck with clarity. I changed and I needed to face that."

"Will you ever do another show again?" Jenn asks.

"No, never ever. It was nice to go back, but the future is what I want to chase. Honestly, I'm lonely. I have the best family in the world, but I need someone to hold me, be there for me. I'm not in any hurry, but I want to start looking."

"It's brave that you can admit that and go for it. You know you will find it." Dana chuckles, "Although, I'm going to keep this all from Axl. He won't like the idea too much."

My son has so much love, just like his dad. I'm grateful he gave me him. "No, let's not bother him with those details." Guilt pinches at my heart for marrying a man so quickly. Axl will be hurt and especially because I never told him. We blurred lines in our relationship that we need to clean up. Over the years, I let him take care of me. He should be more focused on his family.

Ice did hammer it home how much I missed having a man. He sparked me back to life. I craved his touch and attention. It made me happy. Regardless, I need to get back on track and work on the future. "Maybe it's time I get a job. Meeting people and starting over. It would be good for me." Ambition burns bright and I like this plan. Even though it still stings that Ice didn't want me. He never came for me, just a 'we are done' message. I heard it, loud and clear.

"There is always the bar, brewery, or shop you could work in," Dana supplies.

"No, thank you. I want to venture out and spread my wings. Not that I don't appreciate the offer, but I need a change, new scenery, something that is mine. Different." I try my best to explain. What I love is that these girls are my family, and I was afraid for nothing. Even if I did tell them about Ice, they would be supportive. After lunch, we start filling out applications online to department stores

109

and coffee shops, anything that I could start doing. From there, anything could be possible. At least it will also help keep my mind off his intense fire that stroked my desires. The angry man who grabbed my attention and held my life in his hands. Ice, passionate but cold.

TWENTY-TWO

Ice

No sign of Chloe in a week. We are all worried about where she could be, if this is the first string of bad luck. And we were right. Sitting in church, we get a call from our sister clubhouse in Carson City. Grim, the Prez, and his brothers hold a meeting with us. A new ATF agent is looking for Harley in Reno. My gut hits the floor. I assumed that since we separated, no one would know. I spear River a glance, looking for a confirmation that he did annul our marriage.

River shakes his head, telling me that he didn't get the annulment done because we've been hunting down the missing girl from the brothel. River and I aren't saying why they may be snooping around her. They may be checking to see if she knows anything about their missing informant. They may not know she's married to me. But I have only seconds to respond. "Bring her up here."

"Ice, we need to call in the Battle Born. We can't—"Grim tries to refute.

"If you don't, I will. It's not negotiable. Make it look

like she took off. I'll deal with Battle Born, if they can find her." It's irrational and reckless. I should leave her there. Her son can protect her, but it's not good enough. I want to see her face, especially after her last response. We have unfinished business. Maybe one last hate fuck to seal the deal over our divorce papers. Then I'll let her go.

"You better know what the hell you are doing, Ice," Grim states, resolved. "I'm not taking the heat for you on this one. Women are off limits and you know that."

"I know exactly what I'm doing. They owe me. It's a non-issue since we are married." Axl will be pissed off, but I can't seem to find it in me to care.

"Well, fuck me. Allow me to go introduce myself to your misses then."

The secret is most definitely out, and the room is silent with the gaping faces at the bomb I dropped.

Harley

There is a knock at my door. Setting my book down, I peek through the window to find two men from the Royal Bastards at my doorstep. "What the hell?" Instantly, my fuse is lit. Frustration and anger radiate from my body. Swinging the door open, I give them a piece of my mind, "You can tell Ice to go fuck himself. Hand me the divorce papers. I'm done with this shit already." Shooting out my hand palm up, I wait for them to smack the document into my grip so I can get rid of them.

ICE

"Married, you say? Ice did mention that. Gotta say, I didn't believe it and had to see it for myself." One smirks, and now this is starting to make more sense. "Tell me, did you two elope while in Vegas?" His rocker says 'Grim, President'.

"Yes. Why do you care?" I snap back.

"Just curious, and no, I don't have any papers to deliver. We do need to deliver you though."

"Me?" I point at my chest. "What is going on?"

"Apparently, Ice has summoned his wife. He can tell you the rest."

My arms barricade over my chest. "No. Way. Not Leaving."

He sighs, "C'mon, Harley. It's important, or I wouldn't be standing at your door." He holds his finger over his mouth, telling me to be quiet, "He needs to talk with you about your trip."

Chills run down my spine, fear locks me in place, and Grim walks in, gently pushing me back. "You have my word, it won't take long. Pack a bag, we need to get going." At the end, he emphasizes the *get going* part, and suddenly, being alone here doesn't sound so good. Telling Axl what happened sounds even worse. The misogynist in me wants to see Ice and give him a piece of my mind, my side of the story. Nodding my head, the two MC brothers come in while I pack up my dogs and a bag. Wheeling my suitcase out, I get a kick out of their faces and how it drops when they spot Bella and Ben. "Yep, you all get what you asked for." I mentally tap myself on my own back with my head held high. I'm a package deal and don't I know it. "Let's get this pony show on the road." Showing them out, I lock the door, then prepare for the next part, facing off with a cold stone killer who lights up my nerves. My husband, Ice, the President of the Royal Bastards MC.

TWENTY-THREE

Ice

Late in the evening, the party is in full swing, and tits, ass, and grass is all out. You name it, it is smoked, drank, or snorted. I sit at the bar waiting with Jameson in my glass and the bottle next to it. My anxiety is hiked way up. Neither one of us know what will happen once my little fugitive crosses the threshold.

The club girls stay back. They know the fastest way to get their asses kicked out is to approach me first. If I want it, I'll call you over to me. The pissed off glacier stare I am giving to the room also affords me a wide berth to stew alone with my thoughts, a feeling I am not familiar with. My mind tosses back and forth a response to her being here. The uncharted territory proves to me why you never get involved, women are too damn messy.

An SUV pulls up and the lights shut off. Three doors open and close, and at first sight, she smiles brightly, laughing at one of them. Rage snakes through me at how easy and relaxed she is with another man, and a brother. I won't break and show my temper for anyone, until it is time. Now is not it.

ICE

Over the music and party, I listen for the telling sound of the front door opening and shutting, followed by footsteps. I can feel the glacial gaze on my back, but I refuse to submit to her. "Honey, you summoned?" The room goes dead silent from the chatter and laughs, leaving the music blasting in the background. Like a drama queen, she puts on a show. "If you wanted me to sign the divorce papers, you could have sent them with a currier."

Slowly, I turn in my seat and a menacing smirk crawls across my face. Visions of her bent over the bar, taking it up her ass, threads through my brain. She wants to throw down a gauntlet in my house?

"Where's my room, sweetie?" She further coaxes the fire and my patience.

"Take my wife to *our* room." Her face pales just a touch and I stalk over to her, so close we stand nose-to-nose. "Nice to see you too, sweet cheeks. Why don't you go get comfortable and get naked. I'll be in to take care of you in a bit."

Harley's face reddens, but she plays the game well. Snapping my fingers to a prospect, he jumps out from behind the bar to take her bag from Grim and wheels her luggage away. Harley waltzes off with her dogs in tow on a fucking leash. I want to scrub my hands over my face. The yappy frilly mutts excitedly wag their tails, keeping up with her long strides.

In my office, they give me an update that they weren't followed and will head out in the morning. They can't stay, and honestly, I don't know how long she'll be here. I hand them a wad of cash for their troubles. "Grab some food, sleep, whatever you need. Thank you."

"I'm not sure how you let that one leave your sights. Maybe work your shit out," Grim comments.

I grunt in response because I can't keep her. They head into the kitchen and I find my wife waiting for me in my room, seething angry. "What am I doing here?" She points in a large circle around the room, flinging it back down to her side.

"Doing what I need you to do. What the hell was that shit out there, Harley? If you want to push me, go ahead, but don't be surprised when I take control of my clubhouse. One pass, that is your only warning."

"You're an asshole. Everything you do is about you. Maybe you could have called me to let me know that I needed to come here, or I don't know, ask!"

"Funny you mention letting someone know. You left me stranded in Vegas with no way home. I would have a fuck ton of problems if you were hurt."

"I don't need to be babysat. And who cares, you found your own ride home, big deal, Ice. You were going to leave me anyway, may as well be the first to cut than get left behind."

"You left me there. I had no idea what happened to you," I yell in her face.

"I was scared, Ice," she growls back.

"That makes no sense. So you run off alone? They could find you alone, Harley."

"I was scared of you, asshole. Scared about what it meant that I carelessly ran off with you and what you gave me. Terrified that I loved the rush!" she hollers back at me, puffing out each breath. "Then," she jabs a finger into my chest, "you send me a message. You sent the necklace that I

116

loved and a nasty fucking reminder. Why, Ice? If you cared for me, then why not talk to me?"

"Harley, you ran out because I gave you exactly what you asked for. ME! Then I give you more and you ran the hell out like a spineless coward. You left me, remember that," I growl at her. My instincts take over and I grab her. "Are you a chicken shit who can't stand up to our family in Reno and tell them what you really are? *My wife*, who loves it when I give it to her rough and dangerous?"

My hand has her jaw firmly locked in my hold. Harley's eyes start to well with the truth, she was a coward. I need her to know how much she hurt me and I kiss her with all the anger and pain welled up inside. I let it all loose with every twist of my tongue. She is mine and this kiss claims what we are—fire and ice. The constant pull to touch her calls to me. My fingers are digging into her ass, bringing her closer to me. Harley relaxes her body and moans into my mouth. I want it all and take advantage of slipping my tongue around hers, our tongues mingling and taking out our frustrations in our kiss. Fighting for the truth and dominance with this kiss. Except it's no kiss at all. It's a beginning to the end of our fight. I will never say I'm sorry, because I'm not sorry about any of it, and neither is she. We are at a stalemate.

Our bodies agree on one thing, we need to release some of our pent-up tension. Releasing my hold on her ass, I undo her pants first, pushing them down. Our clothes start to fly off in all directions while we maul each other. Once I have her naked, I flip her around, facing my bed. With my hand in her hair, I bend her over. My cock jerks at the site of her pussy.

Excitement fuels the unknown with Harley, never knowing what I will see from her next. I crack my hand across her ass. She howls at the sting of her skin. Two more smacks and she is yelling at me, calling me names I could care less about because they are all true.

"You are my wife, Harley. You can't just walk out," I grit out, sliding my dick into her, calming some of the beast raging inside when she moans. "I didn't release you yet."

"We said it was only lasting a few days!" I barrel into her body, showing her that maybe I changed my mind. She just hasn't got the message yet.

"Shut the fuck up, woman, and take this dick!" My hands grip her hips, pulling her back against me with every thrust.

"Oh, God." She heaves before her body tenses and comes, milking my cock. I explode inside her. My head falls back and I groan while the aftershocks ride through my body, savoring the feel of her hot and wet on my dick.

Slowly pulling out, I admire how her body encases my cock followed by my cum dripping from her swollen lips. Harley falls to the mattress and crawls forward before resting face-down to catch her breath.

Taking the reprieve from our fight, I decide on a hot shower, and I leave Harley alone. In my en suite bathroom, I turn the water on scalding hot and relax under the spray, resting both my hands on the tile in front of me. The glass door slides open and Harley bumps me with her hip to get me out of her way.

Glancing over my shoulder, I wonder how in the fuck she feels so comfortable to waltz into my bathroom and make herself perfectly at home. She is the only woman

who can tame the wild beast from within. Shock or res-
ignation stuns me and I move out the way and watch her
moan and relax in the spot I was just in. Her hair is up
in a bun and she tilts her head back to rinse her neck and
breasts that are hidden from my position.

My eyes trace the water that streams down her back
and legs. Red marks her skin at her hips and ass from my
hands. I take it all in. She uses my soap to quickly rinse off
then pats my cheek on her way out. "Thanks, honey bear."
Harley laughs at herself, then jumps out when I growl, still
cracking herself up while drying off. I grip the soap and do
the same before I turn the water off.

When I walk into the room, she's laying on her side
with Bella and Ben at her feet and yawns. "Turn off the
lights. We can argue tomorrow. I'm too tired to care."

Again, I'm shocked at her carefree attitude. I expected
more resentment or fighting. She looks peaceful here. No
one talks to me this way and not get kicked out. The problem is, I'm starting to believe I don't want her to leave tomorrow or ever.

TWENTY-FOUR

Harley

I lied to Ice.

I pretended I didn't want to talk last night. Truth is, I wanted him to tell me everything and hold me. I can't get attached to him, because he doesn't need anyone. Around dawn, I woke up with our bodies wrapped around each other. Sleeping next to a man does something to a woman in her heart. I realize the importance of this and what it means. I'm falling in love with Ice. Against all odds, I'm letting a part of me and the past go. I'm trusting that I do love my dead husband, but giving myself enough grace to be happy. Believing my heart has enough room. For the longest time, I lived up to the woman I was in Las Vegas. Lived up to the hype of the queen who sat on the biker's lap. She doesn't walk this earth anymore. It's time I man-up, be who I am, and stop living a lie. I will be free and now I know how to do it. I will grow. Very slowly and quietly, I sneak out of his room and take the dogs out to the back yard with a cup of coffee in hand.

"You know he'll just toss your ass aside when he's done with you right?"

ICE

I choke a little on my coffee and crane my head to the right. A gorgeous woman with a sneer stands behind me. She's blonde with a beautiful figure, at least ten years younger than I am. It doesn't surprise me. These guys have a broad range of women they take to bed. "Don't worry about me, I wear big girl panties. If you have something to say, keep it between you and Ice. I don't know you and let's keep it that way."

She huffs, "I'm surprised he brought you back from Las Vegas. I figured he was down there for business, not pussy. Doesn't mean he won't come back to me." She stomps off back to the hole she crawled out of. I'm surprised she's awake at this hour, but maybe she's calling it quits and getting off. I chuckle to myself and ignore the rant of someone I don't even know or care about. I've seen the men of the MC world and how they act. I'm under no delusion that I'm not temporary. Resigned, I focus on what I need to do to get home. Talk to Ice and find out why I am here.

After I finish my coffee, Bella and Ben join me in the kitchen. I pull out eggs and bacon then potatoes. I start to slice and fry the potatoes then cook the bacon and eggs. The aroma of breakfast seems to wake the house up and a few men wander in. Their eyes zero in on my tattoo brand from Maddox and give me a wide berth. They also know I'm married to their Prez.

"Grab the plates and pass me some bowls, please?" The brothers are kind and pass me what I need. The small group sits at the table for a family-style breakfast. We start to plate our food and I ask, "Go ahead and ask." I'm ready to get the awkwardness out of the way.

River gives me his best intimidating look. "Did you really marry the Prez?"

"Yes."

"Are you running from your Ol' Man?"

"Nope, he died a few years back." I suck in a bit of air at the sting. Some words will never be okay, and for me, that is one.

The room falls silent and the demeanor changes a bit, especially when Ice walks in and stumbles when he catches sight of me at a table eating with his men. I start to make him a plate and set it down next to me. He looks between us, uncertainty crossing his face before he brings himself and a black coffee to the table.

"Did you sleep good, sweetie?" Taunting him has become my new favorite pastime. He's such an easy target.

His hand lands on my inner thigh and squeezes. "Remember what I told you last night. I'll spank your ass and then eat my food. Try me, Harley, I'd love it."

Chills run up and down my spine. Leaning into his ear, I rasp, "I may like it too."

The room gets heavy with our threats promised back and forth, but River breaks the moment. "While you two clearly are still in some phase of a honeymoon, let's not be gross in front of the kids. These potatoes are perfect."

Chuckling, I grab a piece of bacon. I thank River and turn to Ice. "So tell me why I am here?" Then I take a bite.

"It can wait a few more minutes, Harley." Ice sounds irritated that I brought it up at the table. Interesting. So he's hiding something from the group. I'll let him have this one, because even though teasing him is fun, I do respect his boundaries as the Prez.

"Sure, pumpkin, we can take the dogs on a walk and catch up." The brothers fight back the grins from crossing their faces, and I promise myself that's the last one when Ice growls and tosses his fork on his plate. "Okay, okay," I hold up my hands in surrender. "Too far. Last one, I promise," I say and cross my heart with a pointed finger and hand him his fork back. Ice rips it from my hand and I bump his shoulder with mine. Storm, his patch says, gives me a thumbs up from across the table. It seems no one is allowed to tease the Prez. That sounds sad and boring to me.

After we eat breakfast, I follow Ice into his office to find it bare. No pictures or mementos of his life, nothing. I sit in a chair across from him. "So, tell me, why did you kidnap me?" My phone was taken away and turned off as soon as I got into the SUV yesterday.

"ATF is looking for you. They've been looking for ways to gather information on you to get you to be their next informant against your son's MC. They need an in."

My head starts to spin. "So why am I here?"

"Because, my dear sweet wife, we are married. And that allows you certain privileges. Like killing agents who poke around something that belongs to me. Also, they'll lose interest, because like I said, you're mine and they'll have to find another way to infiltrate now when you're not so vulnerable."

"Wow," I almost scream. "Hold on a minute. That's why you went with me, why you married me!" I stand and slam my hands on the desk.

"Yes and no. It was convenient to do so at the time. Now that they are snooping further, you need to stay here.

Also, my wife can't testify against me if in the event they figure things out."

"Ice, I realize that doing things as you please is nothing to you, but taking a vow means a lot to me."

"Then why, Harley? I couldn't have made you do it. Maybe who you really are mad at is yourself."

Sitting back down, I calm down. I am big enough to admit the truth. "You may have done it for your reasons. A part of me did it because I was lonely. You can bring out parts of me I didn't know even existed. I trusted you for reasons I don't think I will fully understand in my lifetime. There's no use arguing over what happened. It's done, and don't worry, I realize it's one-sided." The rest I clam up and keep inside. I was honest, there's no reason to spill my guts.

TWENTY-FIVE

Ice

I wasn't expecting her to be honest. What was I expecting her to do? Hide the truth and then we could fight about it until it drew us together? We are like explosive magnets. We draw each other in and then blow up, same cycle on rinse and repeat.

"You need to call Axl and tell him where I am. This won't end well if he has to chase me down," Harley threatens.

"I don't need to do shit. You're my wife. Mine. I'll let Axl know what is going on when he needs to know. Right now, I don't know why ATF was sniffing around so closely. Until I have my answers, I don't see why I need to put you or me at risk."

She glares and stews a second. You can see her talking herself out of ripping into my ass and I wish she would. "Ice," she huffs, "you can't steal a person and run away. They will run all over the state until I am found. You just don't do that to people you care for." Harley walks around the desk and sits in my lap. Her fingers run through my hair.

"Would you at least please call Blade and let him know that I'm here?"

My palms run up her legs and I squeeze her ass. It's the best damn thing I have ever felt in my life, her sweetness. The bitter asshole in me doesn't believe her and I push her away with my words. "Then what, Harley? What will you give me?" If she is going to use me, I'm no fool not to capitalize on it. She wants to bargain, I'm all hers.

"As in, you want me to bend over your desk?" She sounds incredulous.

"Harley, if you want to use your body to get what you want from me, then I will take it. All of it."

Her hand flies for my cheek. I catch her wrists right before impact and snarl, "No one fucking hits me ever."

"I'm not one of your club bitches running around here." She inches closer until our noses almost collide. "I, as your wife, was asking for your help, being that you took my phone and I have a family who will be worried about me. I was talking to you. Say that to me again and I will have no problem finding my way out of here. Alone. Again." Harley tears her wrist free from my grip and pushes herself off my lap.

"Run out of here and I won't come after you." Every word feels like battery acid on my tongue, but it's hard to back down. I haven't had to answer to anyone in a long damn time. That doesn't stop me, not even with the disappointed face she gives me.

"I wasn't asking you to. I can take care of myself, Ice. In case you haven't noticed, I was just fine before you and I will be after you send me packing. Tossing me aside means shit, but caring for me would actually surprise me." Harley turns on her heels and bolts out of my office. The door slams and the wall shakes from her effort. I cringe at the scene and scrunch the beard starting to grow on my jaw.

The few minutes I have alone, I think over her words. Her polite request and sweetness I assumed was a trap to get me to do what she wants. Manipulate me into position. "Fuck," I belt out and run my hand over my head. My whole life, I assumed the worst in everyone, trained to look for weaknesses and lies. I see them everywhere now. I evaluate angles and how I can get on top. In the process, I shoved her aside.

I'm about to get up and check that Harley hasn't packed up and headed for the bus station when there is a knock at the door. River pokes his head in. "Prez?" Once he sees me, I flag him in. Shutting the door, he stumbles a moment. "It appears your wife wants either a room with, I quote, *'your club bitches or whores'*. She is packing her stuff and said she will meet me in the main room in five."

"Are you fucking kidding me?" I growl.

River shakes his head no then grins. "You are in the doghouse. Good luck with that one. Where should I put her? If she goes to the—" He doesn't have to finish. The girls who are sent to the Stable or with the club girls housing are free to fuck anyone and that doesn't sit right. It doesn't matter the fight we had, she's not leaving. I just need to figure out how to fix this.

"Go to my room and tell her she can stay in there. I'll find another room."

"Ice, go to her."

"Mind your own business, River. My woman, my

problem." I won't negotiate for a second time today. It's done and over with. She'll take that and get the hell over her little tantrum. I'll deal with her when I can. For now, I need to figure out how ATF was down there. Almost like it wasn't a surprise that I was there. Usually, a handler wouldn't risk being seen with their moles. They changed up the normal routine and I need time to figure out what I am missing.

"Take care of Harley and get back in here with Storm. Something is off." He leaves with a nod of his head, agreeing. I need a few moments to think. I have no such luck when there is a small rap on the door, alerting me to incoming company. I wouldn't be surprised to see any of the brothers walk in, not the woman who strolls in. The blonde has curves that men dream of and a face to get lost in while her lips are wrapped around your cock. She sashays over to my desk in skimpy black lingerie. Small scraps of fabric cover her nipples and pussy from view.

Any other man would be powerless and bow to her, eat her pussy, and get lost in her luscious breasts. Tina was made for fucking. That's it. She knows coming into my office is not permitted for any of the girls, ever. They are not to try and seduce me. This is an example of why I find women to be lying and scheming bitches I have always known them to be.

She runs a hand over my arm and shoulder. Another no. Inside, I want to boil over and kick her out, but my gut tells me to wait. She has never demonstrated this behavior before. She either is fighting for dominance over Harley, rejecting her place in the stables, or something I have missed altogether. I push my knee jerk reaction aside and watch.

ICE

"I'm due to work again tonight." Her throaty rasp is filled with intrigue and want. "I thought you might have free time. I could help take care of you first." She sets her ass on my desk and lays across the surface. Her breasts in direct line with my body. "I've missed our time together. I'll share you. Whatever you need, I'll give." Her finger dances across my chest.

My hand darts out and I hold her wrist. "What is it you need from me, Tina?" I grit the words out through my clenched jaw. My patience is about to snap. I could break her wrist for touching me in one quick twist.

"You. We were so close and shared so much. I need more, to know more about you."

"Hmmm." I think over her words. Whispers of desire we have never shared. She knew the score and is now lying. I give her what she wants temporarily until I dig up more information. "I'll call on you when I'm ready for you. Get out." Abruptly, I stand and pull her up from her position on my desk. Tina stumbles to find her footing in her fuck-me heels. I don't stop, pulling her forward to the door and yanking it open. There is only so much I can take and my patience is gone.

Down the hallway, Harley watches us emerge from my office. Her arms cross over her chest with pursed lips. These two can deal with their own female shit. I have bigger shit to deal with. With Tina out of my office and Harley glaring at me from down the hallway, I let Tina's wrist go and duck back into my office, slamming the door in my wake of anger.

This is why bitches become liabilities, distractions from your job and keeping your men alive. They have a purpose and that is to spread their legs and keep their bullshit to themselves. I don't want it. One thing that will happen by the end of the night is Tina will find out who the man is she crossed. Her fate is determined by what we find.

TWENTY-SIX

Harley

I f you could explode from hate and disgust, I would in this second. I hate Ice, he's an egotistical, emotional inept ass. He seriously has a club girl, or whore, in his office, showing the crude and vile man underneath. A possessive streak I have never felt before comes out front and center. It makes me sick to think that I want to be his, and only his, when I think all those other things about him. What have I become? Am I really that lonely? I would say hell no, but it makes no sense to me.

Tina looks satisfied with her appearance. Nothing I haven't seen before. Men in this life take what they want, when they want it. It's nothing new when they step out on their girlfriends or Ol' Ladies. Clearly, Ice is the same. She smirks and cocks a hip out to talk shit and bring me down to her level. I'm too old for that shit and march on past. "Save it, bitch. Fuck him or whatever. I don't need anyone that bad, like you." Her shoulder bumps into mine on her way past. I've never hit a woman, but she may just be the first. I let her go as tempting as the thought may be.

When I round the corner, I bump into Storm, who was perched there eavesdropping. "Hey, firecracker, slow down. You want to get the Prez back?" he whispers with an edge of conspiracy. "Dig out a bikini and tan in the backyard."

Glaring back at the man I have only spoken with a few times, I contemplate his angle. "Something tells me that would cause more problems than I would ever want. If Ice wants to be a dumbass, I have no interest in stopping him."

"Good to know. Carry on and kill, firecracker." Storm grins.

"Storm," River hollers. "Need you in the office." He steps around me, whistling down the hallway on his way. Frustrated and angry, I head to their small gym. After some stretching and selecting the perfect playlist, I hit the treadmill. I've always been a runner, and in high school, I was offered a scholarship to college for track. Growing up in Vegas, the spotlight was too bright to resist and started modeling. It brought me to where I am and I will never regret it.

It floats through my mind that had I gone, I would have met a different man. One who worked eight to five. I would have likely married a teacher or a lawyer. Would I have been happy? I don't think I would. The club always afforded me that bite of excitement in life I craved. Ice, though, his fierce crushing bluntness is brutal at times. Parts of me crave to be with the beast, owned by a force so powerful, it would be indescribable.

My body pushes itself with each step on the treadmill. Blood pumps harder through my veins from the idea of Ice's hand around my throat while he powered into me. I fought to stay conscious that night. The freeing feeling between life and death in his fingertips. I never came so hard in my life. Seeing stars took on a whole new meaning.

Why him? Why do I want that? His domineering possessive behavior. It's comforting when for so long I felt like the world was floating by. Why I need that now, I don't understand. Each step, I push myself physically but also mentally. I try to process the change in my world. Nothing makes sense but also feels so right at the same time. And it all has to do with the man who made me see the world, my world, differently.

I never considered myself to be a woman who needed a man to complete her. That is not true, I find now. I crave the relationship of two souls. A partner to give me direction, his ruthless convictions draw me in. I can't help but want to fall to my knees and look to him. He completes that desire deep down that I have hidden away. Ice is the piece that snaps me into place.

What I worry the most over is do I do that for him. Am I that piece that he wants in his life? If given the chance to be loved by a man like him, I couldn't turn it away. I just don't know that he can love me in return.

TWENTY-SEVEN

Ice

Storm found a burner phone in Tina's belongings. There are texts back and forth to an unknown number with dates and times. All of my whereabouts in the last week. It's enough to tell me she's been feeding ATF information for who knows how long. When she got tied up with them, I will find out.

The three of us rode over to the stables after more digging into her life. She has a dealer she owes a lot of money to, not to mention she is late on payments. I will make it clear to him to stay away from my club girls. In that, he won't be breathing in the next few hours.

Swinging the front door open, the girls are alerted to attention. Hopeful eyes scan us, wanting to play with the big boys who cut their checks. If I fucked them before, I don't go back for seconds. I can't say the same for Storm. The bastard winks at them as we pass the ones at the bar waiting for their Johns to show up for the night and collect their commissions.

River and Storm settle at the bar. I head to the back

room and pound on the door assigned to Tina. Slowly, she opens it until she sees me on the other side. Tina swings it wide open, naked and freshly showered.

"Hey, baby. I'm ready for you."

It's on the tip of my tongue to ask her if one dick isn't enough for her but hold it back. "Shut the fucking door," I bark. She slams it shut and gets on all fours, like I trained her to do, to be my bitch when I need to fuck. "Sit the hell down. I don't want your used pussy in my face."

Tina whips around, scared and confused. She should be. "What have you been saying about me, to who and for how long?"

"Ice, c'mon, you know I wouldn't betray you." Tina tries to play off the carefree, innocent girl act, but I know better. "I did-n't," she stutters. "I woul-d-n't—"

Gripping a handful of her hair, I rip her head back and penetrate her teary regretful eyes. "Every lie is making it worse for you. Who, and how long?"

She swallows, clearing the lies she was ready to spew at me. "He figured out you were covering for Battle Born. He needed leverage on the members to bust them." She clams up the rest of the truth and holds back what she wanted to confess.

My hand sliced across her face. She was unable to fly with the impact. My hold rips her hair at the back of her head. Bringing my face close, I snarl, "You are going to die, Tina. You better get to talking."

"He told me that if I didn't help, I would go to jail for the drugs he planted in my house and blackmail me for trafficking charges. If I didn't do it, he would take you down too. I thought I was saving you," Tina pleads with her life.

It's too late. She betrayed me, putting my brothers and myself at risk. Had she told me, I may have respected her that much more. I would have cut her out of the club completely, but she would have lived. "I don't have time to explain to you how stupid you are. If he was blackmailing you, he had nothing. You're a weak pawn who knows too much."

I could let her go. The chances are she would exploit her knowledge for money and revenge. Tell a rival club or connect with the agent and he would be a ghost in the wind. There is only one choice. Clean it up. "Call or text him, where you two normally meet and time." My eyes drill into hers. She knows her torture will be gruesome if she defies me.

Her body shakes like a leaf as she sends him a text to meet her tomorrow morning at a small casino just outside of town. Tina hands me the phone and promises me the moon. "It won't happen again, Ice, I swear."

"No, Tina, it won't." Her body sags in relief. Pocketing her phone, I grip her hair at the top of her head. Forcing her to stand, I spit into her face. "I would fuck your ass raw, but there isn't a chance in hell my dick would touch you."

She squirms in my hold, kicking and screaming to get away. No one will come for her to save her. I drag her the length of the room along with me out to the main room. The temperature drops to a cold chill. The girls scatter away, making room for the commotion heading their way. My hold is fierce on her hair. Tina cries and begs me to stop, her naked body shuddering in fear.

"Storm, cover the front." He locks the doors and River stands at the opposite end of the room from me. "Nobody moves." My words sound like venom. "This is your only warning from me. You betray the men of this club, the dicks you love so much sliding into your wet greedy little cunts, you die by that hand."

Tina howls out, "No, stop, please!" Her kicking and scratching becomes even more frantic. The steel blade in my other hand meets her neck at her jugular.

"Shut the fuck up, rat." With those parting words, I press forward at an agonizing pace. A blood curdling scream is followed by the gurgling sound of her choking on her own blood. Her hands hold her throat desperately, her wild eyes darting around the room. Ripping the knife away from her throat, Tina's knees give in and I let her drop like a sack of potatoes. Her body quivers, then stops. The silence is a call from the devil.

Looking around the room, some of the girls cry and cover their eyes, and some can't look away from the horrific scene. Pointing the bloody blade at the room, I make eye contact with them all. "You whisper one word about club business to anyone, or talk about this day, you will be the next one laying cold and bleeding on the floor. Clean this up." My voice is resigned but my body is tight with a manic rage. Tina could have harmed my brothers or Harley. None of that will ever be acceptable. It's not the first bitch I've murdered or tortured and won't be the last. I've never seen loyalty in a woman last longer than her orgasm.

TWENTY-EIGHT

Ice

"**W**ho, motherfucker, did you think you were messing with?" My fist connects with the asshole who has been selling drugs to Tina. He flies off the barstool at the local casino and bar. No one will help him or stop me. I run the northeastern territory, everything that happens here belongs to me and the people in it.

Savage.

River and Storm pick him up from off the floor. I toss the bartender a few hundred-dollar bills on the bar top while he is dragged back to the storage room. Voices pick back up and heads turn back to mind their own business. No one saw anything. What guy? My boots thunder on the floor after them. A handful of brothers stay back and sit at the bar to keep a lookout.

Their shoulders push the back doors open and the little puke is tossed on the floor. From my pocket, I drag out and flip open my switchblade. He rolls over and groans on his back before he starts to cough. "I didn't know."

ICE

Frustrated as all fuck, I kick the asshole in the ribs. The crack of his bones crumble under my black steel-toe boots. He heaves and rolls over, coughing. I stomp out more of my frustration on him. Too much is pent up from Harley. The indecision of where she and I stand makes me feel out of control. My nerves crawl with need, and if I can't hate fuck her, I'll torture the fuck out of him. This, I can control, and drain some of the lingering stress.

After several more punishing kicks, I quit. I still need him conscious for the next part. My foot digs into his shoulder to push him onto his back. Squatting low, I hold the blade under his chin. "Why did you target her?" I could give two fucks it was Tina, the why is important.

"I was paid to get her to use, giving her more and more. Close enough to where I could plant drugs on her when I was called." ATF was using this guy to do their dirty work, keeping their hands clean. The point of the knife digs into his skin. A small droplet of blood trickles down his throat, my eyes tracking it, the enticing urge to spill it all capturing my attention.

"Anyone else?"

"Just her for now, unless you picked a new woman." Which I had. Harley can't leave. ATF will be relentless to get her. They never will. My wrist snaps away and the blade swings back into itself. In one fluid motion, I pocket it, then wrap his head into my hold. One quick snap to the side and his neck breaks. You can feel his last breath as it escapes his body.

"Dump him out back," I instruct while emptying his pockets. "Call Cal and have him dispose of the body as usual." Cal owns the garbage company. He'll burn the body

139

and bury him deep under the landfill, never to be found again. Storm is on his phone while River heaves the lifeless man over his shoulder. Clean and over.

I toss Storm his phone and wallet to erase the man from the earth. If he has no connections, it will be as if the man was never even born. If he has connections, then they will be evaluated as a possible threat. You kill one man, you end up killing their whole family, if that is the case.

It doesn't take River long and the brothers follow me out to the next meeting point. How desperate is the ATF agent? Will he meet Tina? If he was halfway good at his job, he would be gone, a ghost. In the parking lot, we halt before climbing onto our bikes. "I need you all to spread out, scour the city. Look for the hole he's been hiding in. If you find him, call me. That's it." In case he plans on leaving, I send them out on a manhunt.

The bikes rumble to life. The power of the engines vibrate our ribs and hearts. The power of the brotherhood shines bright in the darkness. We hunt, find, and kill. No one touches what belongs to me, and that includes Harley, whether I am ready to admit that or not. She's not leaving this city without me at her side. Harley has made my fantasy and dreams to control her reality. For the first time, my soul is whole and I will paint the state red to protect her. Damn Battle Born or ATF if they think they will stand in my way. All along, I thought I was going to show her what it was like to be set free of her mind, but in reality she set me free.

For hours, we ride around looking for possible traces of the man, and as I suspected, he hasn't been spotted. Both good and bad news. Good that he never made it that close. Bad because I had to chase him down when he was under my nose the whole time. I don't want to explain my business to anyone ever, unless absolutely necessary. Giving up my search, I back off and head to the meet-up point, minus my cut. The small casino in Carlin, east of Elko, is quiet in the early morning. The sun rises over the horizon and I park my bike.

My body protests from being up all night. The high to find the agent was my number one priority and kept me awake. But after my first step off my bike, my body tells me otherwise. Miles of road are now chasing and slowing me down. I'm not some young fucker chasing the world anymore. The idea of settling between Harley's thighs at night sounds more like my speed. This old dog still has bite.

At a small counter bar, I take a seat and wait to see if I'll get lucky today. A cup of coffee is slid across to me. From my seat, I can see River and Storm smoking outside of the side of the building, out of view of the parking lot. There is no doubt if he spots our faces, he will be in the wind. It's a shot in the dark, but it's also all I have. This ends now. This is the last kill for Battle Born, our contract is up.

A blacked-out unmarked sedan pulls into the parking lot. I turn in my seat, holding up the local paper while sipping my coffee. Pulling out my phone, I dial River. "Looks like we have a pick-up this morning."

"I'll keep a tail, meet you at the shop," River replies then hangs up. Nothing will happen here. He's safe for a few more minutes. The surprising fact is the man who walks in can't be more than twenty-five. Must be a new recruit they got to take on the shit jobs. Too bad for this kid. I sip my coffee and relax into my seat, reading about the local senior graduates. He scopes out the area and when he is satisfied his little rat is nowhere to be found, he takes off. Spooked, his gut feeling telling him to run, survive. There is no escaping the Royal Bastards.

He's marked as an enemy and will die. The door swooshes open and closes behind me. "Did you want any food?" the young waitress asks.

"Nah, sweetheart. Heading out, back home to Utah." I wink and dazzle her with a fake smile. I roll up the paper and tuck it under my arm. The bikes thunder to life outside, and I can hear them leave the parking lot. "I've got work to do, but maybe next time."

I drop the mask as soon as I exit the casino and race down the highway until the taillights of the sedan can be seen. The car chase is on. He knows and does his best to escape. It was over before it started. Hitting the gas, I let the engine open to full throttle and chase them down. The agent swerves over to the far left and then right to keep us behind him.

River pulls out his gun and fires a round through the back window. The glass shatters and sprays all over the road and back into our face. I cover my face with my elbow the best I can. Storm aims and hits his right front tire when he turns sharp in that direction. The car loses its traction and swerves violently until it's over. The car is spinning out of control and flipping on its top. The sand creates a thick curtain flying in the air around us. I pull up my bandana over my mouth so I can breathe.

ICE

Our bikes screech to a stop. With our guns drawn, we find him hanging upside down in the car, his seatbelt holding him captive. Blood pours down his face. He gurgles, trying to breath, suffering to stay alive. At the back of the car, gasoline drips from the punctured tank. Taking a smoke from River, I light the end, holding it between my thumb and forefinger. The cigarette is lit and a few deep drags are taken before I flick it into the gas. We run to our bikes and skid out of there.

A few seconds pass and the blast chases us down the road. The heat licks at our backs and the explosion threatens to take us with him. You can't kill a man who dabbles in the dark. The devil isn't ready for my soul, not today.

TWENTY-NINE

Harley

An uneasy feeling creeps up into my stomach, an ache I haven't felt in a long while. Something tells me Ice is out working and it's not good. They all sped out of here on a mission. I saw the ambition in their eyes. Something is wrong. I was pissed at him earlier and welcomed the reprieve, but now, I worry about what he is up to. There is no doubt in my mind that whatever it is, it's dangerous. I pray to myself for his safe return. That's when reality punches me in the gut with the truth. I've loved and lost and now I fear what I never thought was possible. I love Ice and need him to come back. We still have so much to learn about each other and I want the time to hear his stories. He is the opposite of what I knew or believed about love. Ice doesn't have the sweet words or overly large gestures.

He could have called Blade, the Battle Born President, and told him the agents were after me. Why didn't he want to do that? It makes sense to keep things open between them, unless he thought if they knew, it would put me at risk. His words were cruel, but I missed the purpose because I was angry.

I think over everything I have known about the man. The occasions we were brought together before. I remember the hidden deep stare Ice had, daring me not to look away and I never could. Back then, I was too drawn into my circumstances to pay attention to the intensity. But now, I can see it. His possessive desire the moment I shut the car door when we left on our trip. Ice looked after everything I needed, even though he was working. Ice doesn't do anything he doesn't want to, but he kept me at his side. He showed me my heart was alive and the dark desires he brought to life.

How in this universe was I fated to become the opposite I knew myself to be? I changed. The darkness of loss twisted something deep inside. He saw it, the change in me, and recognized his match. Did he know all along that he wanted me and held out? Bated his time before the opportunity to strike when it was hot? It wouldn't surprise me that he knew exactly how to manipulate the outcome.

I've always heard that love is love, no matter what form it comes in. It can be different and ever-changing. The real question is, can I see my life this drastically changed? Would Ice keep me here as more than just the woman who warms his bed, or his queen at his side?

His power makes me want to submit to his feet. To give him control of my body and life. Something that I have never felt. The bite of the darkness is a tempting treat and he is the gatekeeper. Will Ice ruin me in the end?

Sleep evades me all night, alone in his bed. My hand covers the pillow where he slept before. His scent surrounds me. I think about all *if*'s and *but*'s all night, tossing and turning, wondering if my reaction to him was right. The stubborn me says he's an asshole and deserved it. The other side says he's never had a woman to show him. How else would he respond? Can I deal with his blunt nature and crass words? Truth is, I'm looking for reasons to fight. I want him to chase after me. Prove that he cares for me. If I don't stop, I'll lose him for good. This I know.

The dogs stir in their beds and I decide to take them out. The fresh air will hopefully calm my racing mind. The mountains here are different than in Reno. A change in scenery is welcome, making it feel like a fresh start. I miss Axl, Dana, and my grandbaby Maddy though. It makes me chuckle to think of Ice with Maddy. She's as sarcastic and feisty as Axl.

In the kitchen, I start a pot of coffee and sit at the table, reading my Kindle. I've done lockdowns numerous times and plan on being here a long time. I've learned to never forget your books or die of boredom. Time flies by while I whip through the pages. The clubhouse is a skeleton crew of what it normally is until members begin to trickle in.

Sitting on the couch, I wait and watch for Ice to come home. I do notice that Storm and River are gone also. If that is the case, he's doing something important. Having them with him makes me feel a fraction better. I try to read the funny story waiting for me to get wrapped up in it. But it is impossible. I can't concentrate. My anxiety has skyrocketed too much to relax. With each sound, I search for him.

Finally, Ice stumbles in with heavy feet. Dark circles

weigh down his droopy, tired, bloodshot eyes. I don't sing out his name, but my heart does. It hammers in my chest and my body relaxes with a long exhale of relief. He's safe and came home. That's all I needed was to see him walk through those doors unscathed.

Ice turns in the direction to his room. My heart sinks when he doesn't look for me, my eyes darting to my Kindle so the others don't see the disappointment. His feet stop and with his back to me, he hollers, "Harley, get your ass in my bed where you belong. If I'm there, you better be naked and waiting for me. Move."

My. Mouth. Hangs. Open.

"Did I stutter?" He slightly turns, his face showing no humor. I comply, my disappointment washed away at the chance to give him what he wants—me. With ease, I hold my composure and walk to him and grumble, "Asshole."

A hand slaps my ass. I yelp with the sting and hustle down the hallway. Note to self, don't call him names. It was no love tap either. That was a boss smack. Ice didn't mess around. I rub my cheek all the way into the bathroom.

I turn the shower on for Ice and help him strip out of his clothes, tossing them into the hamper. I turn to get his boots when he catches my wrist, tugging me to his chest, his nails digging into my ass cheeks. Ice's lips devour mine. Demanding and full of desire, he doesn't let go of the connection until he makes his point, my body is his.

He pulls back. "Harley, you can never have a regular life. Once you're in, it's for life. Why not me, why not us?"

I hesitate, his words throwing me off. Our eyes do all the talking. The thoughts I had earlier came back full force. He probably won't ever say the words, but I know I was right.

He waited for us. It may have not been intentional, but he knew. Ice is a killer and a twisted dark man, but he's mine.

Kissing the corner of his mouth, I wrap my arms around his strong body. He gives me what I need when I ask for it. "Ice, I wouldn't be standing here if I didn't feel what you did." That's when it dawns on me. I need to take as much as he does, when I want it. Backing away, I shred my clothes off and slide my naked body between the sheets. Sitting up in bed, I wait. I give him my submission and do as he asks.

He hesitantly steps into the shower, making quick work of washing the road and elements off him. Ice steps out of the shower dripping wet. He dries off his skin with fast passes of the towel and tosses it aside before making his way to me naked. I soak in the sight. Yes, we are older, but his body is trim and hot.

Ice rips the blanket away from me, the action making my body shiver from the breeze. I crawl over to him and raise to my knees on the mattress. My hands roam over his body and tattoos. This is the first time he has ever allowed me to touch him.

His hand wraps around my neck and tugs me to look at him. "Will you die for me?" His jaw is tight and the words a hiss.

"Only by your hands," I rasp from the pressure at my throat.

"You belong to me. Never, will you be free from me. You will wear my brand. I don't give a fuck about our vows. My Ol' Lady dies at my side."

"I'll die for you, Ice." I mean every word. He scans my face, needing to see the truth in my heart on my face.

His hand flexes and my body responds to his demand

to submit to him. "I'll die protecting you, Harley. Until my last breath, you belong here, as mine." His other hand snakes down and rubs my clit. That is his *I love you*. As long as I have *this*, it will be enough.

My breathing grows labored with every stroke to my pussy. Every pass is a recurrence of what I was already thinking. The darkness brought me to him. My dark king stole me and took me away from myself and brought me back to life. My nerve endings ignite and my body explodes into a fever.

I gasp and rock my hips into his hand. His lips claim mine and absorb the pleasure that sounds from deep in the back of my throat. Ice's teeth pull at my bottom lip. Suddenly, he tears his mouth away from mine. He tosses me back onto the bed and covers my body with his.

Ice's rock-hard cock slides into my slick folds with force, his hips slamming into mine. Ice powers into me over and over again, using my body to bring him pleasure. Wrapping my legs around him, I angle my hips to meet his thrusts, needing more for myself. Both of us are greedy with lust.

The buildup is so close but not enough. I lick my fingers and massage my clit at a furious pace to catch up. With each stroke, a tingle runs up my spine until my body tenses and I come, my pussy clenching around his dick.

Ice groans and has no choice to come with me. His hand holds my jaw as he fucks my mouth with his tongue. My body relaxes and sleep calls my name. Ice rolls over and I groan at the loss of his cock, our connection.

I roll into him and possessively wrap my arms and legs around him. My wet pussy dripping with his cum is paradise. I fall asleep in seconds with him at my side until death do us part as we vowed.

THIRTY

Ice

I don't know how long I am asleep for. It feels like I died, I'm out so deep. My back is stiff and aches, pulling me from my unconsciousness. Harley lays on her side in front of me. This time, I'm wrapped around her.

From this position, I can see the brand on her right shoulder, a heart with the words 'Mad Max, from this life to the next, our love has no bounds' with vibrant red roses and black leaves that intertwine around a black and grey skull with a crown. Loyal even after his death. It doesn't stop me from wanting to consume her. Steal some of that for myself, even though I will never deserve it. I will claim the second half of her life as my own.

Ideas surface of the brand I want here on her left shoulder blade. My name and the MC Logo. My finger traces over the virgin skin. Our pasts are just that, I want what comes next and no one will stop me.

My daydream is interrupted as the roar of several bikes pull into the compound. My instincts tell me something is off. It's as if the air has changed and the threat of survival is floating through it. The shift of my weight when I get out of bed stirs her awake.

"I'm just checking out the clubhouse since we've been out." Pulling on a pair of jeans, I slide on my boots and walk out. The sounds from the room are not from any normal visitors. Blade, Axl, and the Battle Born men stand in the main room. Scorned faces trace my movements as I come their way.

Axl's furious gaze holds my impassive one. I knew he would be pissed. I had intended on going to him soon, there just wasn't time. On the other hand, his mom isn't in any danger. Holding up a hand, I point to my office. My business doesn't need to be aired in front of the clubhouse. They both follow me inside, along with River joining the meeting.

The door slams shut and rattles on the hinges. Inwardly, I smirk because Harley did that not twenty-four hours ago. "Let's calm the fuck down before someone ends up on their ass. I don't barge into your clubhouse and throw my weight around."

"It's more than that," Blade bites. "You care to fill us in, brother, on what the fuck you haven't been?"

"ATF did target Harley down in Vegas. She got home and as soon as I heard they were still tracking her, I had my men pick her up and bring her here. If I would have told you, it could have complicated the situation."

"What motherfucking situation would that be?" Axl growls. "I can take care of her."

"Did you know they were already in Reno? You didn't notice how many hours she was missing. Neither did they. I protected her. They didn't know where to find her. It was the best plan. So fuck off."

Axl charges me like a bull without thought. He doesn't know the extent of it. He will, soon enough. I brace for the impact. His fists fly for my face. I dodge the first two swings, but his fist connects with my stomach. I shove him away from my body, ready to swing. My arm flexes, but I stop.

Harley barges in and the door swings, banging against the wall. "For fuck's sake, enough with the door!" I shout.

"What did you just say?" Axl's anger renews, wanting blood this time. He shoves me with all his weight, but I hold firm and grip his cut.

"Don't think you can come here and stir shit up."

"Fuck you, Ice." He rips himself free of my hold. "We'll be out of your hair. Stay clear of her."

A manic laugh leaves my lungs. "She's mine, Axl. Harley is my wife. She stays here with me."

Harley intakes a sharp breath when Axl spins and glares at his mom. "Is he telling me the truth?" His voice was deathly quiet and defiant. She nods once to confirm. "You married him? You're that desperate for attention?"

Harley snaps at his comment and faces off with her son. Her slap rings across the room. Tears well in her eyes, but she never loses her backbone. "My life is mine. You will not disrespect me or Ice. Take a ride and clear your head. I don't want to see you until you've calmed down." She backs up a step and opens the door. Axl barges past Blade and stops right in front of his mom.

"I never thought, you of all people, would do this, to our name, forget who you are."

"No, Axl, I finally found who I am. It's time for you to go." She holds firm, but I can see her hands tremble. Harley keeps her composure in a breaking moment.

ICE

Axl turns to me. "Meet me at the shaft, one hour." His fierce glare says it all, he wants me dead. Blade keeps me in his view as he leaves my office, not sparing Harley any respect on his way out. As soon as the bikes roar to life and leave the clubhouse, that first tear falls. I hold my hand out for her and she comes to me.

Wrapping my arms around her tightly, I absorb the pain pulsating from her in waves. Each crushing one I welcome because I caused all of this. I kept her here on purpose when she asked me to call them, knowing they would come get her. I didn't want her to leave. "I'll fix it." And I will.

I don't take all of my men with me to our meeting spot deep in the opening of the old mine shaft in the hills. Only River rides with me. I would have loved nothing more than to blow up their skulls with bullets, but Harley stops me. She changed my life. Our game of cat and mouse changed the game of how I play life. It started with me finding and ending men who threatened our lives and protecting my club and ended with me protecting her at all costs.

On the ride up to the mountain, I think about the best approach. Axl is angry and pissed off to hell and back. He wants a fight to prove to Harley I'm a sick son of a bitch. He doesn't need to do that to prove it. I am a sick bastard. I don't give a fuck about them. Winning Harley is the key and I angle my position to do that.

Rolling up in the truck, River asks, "What do you want me to do?"

"Keep Axl alive. If I lose my shit, just keep him alive." River nods, concerned how this could play out. We exit the truck and enter the dark with just the headlights illuminating the area. "Whatever happens after today, you will respect Harley, or never set foot in my clubhouse again. Either one of you. If you think you can come up here and scare me away, you're dead wrong. I'll paint the world red to keep her at my side and we all know that's the truth."

"Do I," Axl smarts. "You love pussy. As soon as you're done with her, you'll toss her aside and throw her into the Stables like all your other bitches. That shit is not happening."

"She's too fucking good for that shit. I'm branding her. Harley is riding with me. She belongs to the Royal Bastards whether you are okay with it or not." With each word, I step closer, showing Axl I'm here and not leaving.

He reaches behind him, pulling out a knife. Just as quickly, I pull mine. We hold each other with our blades at each other's throats. Blood threatens to spill as I grip my knife tighter. Everything I mentioned to River about keeping Axl alive is forgotten. I crave his soul as much as he does mine. Red is all I see.

Blade moves in close. "Axl, step back," he coaxes. "One of you will—"

Axl lunges. I swing to the side, his knife slicing into my arm. I roar and can taste the thrill of the kill in the air. Pushing forward, I'm inches away from burying my blade into his chest when a strong arm wraps around my throat. I pull forward to shake the man off, his arm crushing my throat. Twisting the blade around in my hand, I bury it into his leg before I go out.

154

THIRTY-ONE

Harley

"**A**re you kidding me, Axl! If I didn't slap you already today, I would do it now. You pulled a knife on Ice? What the hell is wrong with you?" My cheeks heat up and burn with how angry and frustrated I am. "Then River has to choke Ice to save you from—"

"Your husband stabbed me in the hand," he growls back at her.

"River got thirty stiches from the stab wound he got from Ice in his leg. You have a Band-Aid on yours."

His face falls in disbelief. River laughs from the couch. "Quit your bitchin', Axl, it's just a Band-Aid. I took the hard hit for you." He's hopped up on pain pills and laughs to himself. "Ice made me promise to get you out of there alive no matter what. It's all good, shit happens." He yawns. "Ice fell for Harley." River's eyes start to flutter then he's out like a light, snoring with a bottle of Jack in hand.

The room falls silent. My skin tingles and I turn to Ice to find he is wearing a murderous gaze on his VP for spilling. I forget all about chewing into my son and slide into a stool next to Ice. My fingers graze over the bandage covering the cut. I place a kiss over it on his bare skin. I notice his cut has a small scrape in the leather from it also. I try to wipe the mark away, wishing Ice's cut hadn't been harmed or any of the men.

"It had to be sorted out. That's nothing, doll, don't worry over it." He keeps his attention on me. His kind words and actions take me on a tailspin. I badly want to tell him I love him. We haven't said those words, instead, I hold his jaw in my hands, his beard rough to my skin. "Thank you for keeping Axl safe." He knew he would hurt him and asked River to back my son. My lips take his this time. It's not overly passionate with lust but demanding with my gratitude. I kiss my way over to his ear and rasp, "You're sexy as fuck, Ice." I mean every word. I would do dirty-dirty things to him right now if Axl wasn't here. "I need a minute to talk with my son. I'll be right back."

"Axl," I stall a moment. "I'm not leaving Ice. I need to talk with you, alone. Will you go with me outside?"

Axl's stare ping-pongs between the two of us. "Are you kidding me? Mom, Ice of all guys. You don't know what you are walking into with him."

"Axl, it's none of your business."

"Really, so your phone being off, me not knowing where my mom is, is none of my business?"

I tense, growing frustrated, because I asked Ice to call Blade. "I apologize you didn't get that. You're right to be upset about that. But, you don't need to get into my personal life."

"What about when your personal life affects the rest of us?"

"Who I'm with is not your problem."

"Jesus." Axl runs his hand through his hair. "Get your stuff. I'll drive you home. We can talk in the truck." Axl's body is tense and vibrates with anger. It's not easy to get him so riled up emotionally. I also know the root of it, he is scared of losing me too after his dad.

"Axl, I'm going to ask you one more time to get your ass outside, or this is over, now." His jaw grinds back and forth, wanting to argue. I'm grateful when he doesn't and follows me outside. He sits in a chair and stays quiet. Of which, I needed a moment to find my words.

"Nothing in life stays the same. Even when we desperately want it too," I start, gazing out to the horizon where the sun sets behind the mountains. "I'm not going anywhere, Axl. Nothing can keep me from you. I'll be your mom always and Maddy's grandma."

"Mom, it's not just that. I've seen the things that Ice has done in revenge for the club. It's...he's...a dark man. I'm worried about you."

"Axl, I've changed. Since your father died, I don't see the world the same as I used to. Everything has changed. Ice has helped me to be okay with who I am. At the house in Reno, I was just surviving. I didn't recognize the person I became. I just felt like I was pretending to be the woman who lived in that house."

"Just come home and we'll figure all this out," he pleads, frustrated.

"No." I turn and hold his stare. "With Ice, I am different. I feel free and I'm not leaving him. I understand his dark side, the man who kills, the monster inside. I'm not a young girl, I know exactly who the man is that sleeps next to me, and I don't want the details. Let it go."

Axl groans in disgust and looks away, avoiding that I am a woman and not a grandma who closed up shop once his dad passed. "We eloped in Vegas. Technically, we are married," I add, wanting to get the rest out of the way.

He abruptly stands and the chair skids back on the wood, renewing his anger. "What in the hell happened in Las Vegas?" he shouts and his hand points to some abstract place.

"Nothing we will talk about. Like I said, we are married. It's done. If you want club answers, you know who to ask for those."

Axl looks around through the glass and must find what who he's looking for. A few seconds later, Ice meets him outside. "You married my mom, and we both know in this world that doesn't mean shit." He spits. "All I need is a retarded little Ice for a brother running around here. Mom, seriously, with your age!"

"Axl, enough of your shit. Know your place with me. I do not owe you anything," Ice bites back. "But I will give you this—I'll do what I want on my own time with Harley. If I want to brand her tonight, it will happen. When she is ready. How long before you branded Dana?"

I start to laugh out loud at the absurdity of their fight. It's gotten ridiculous and out of control. "Axl, go home to Dana and Maddy. Take a few days to absorb everything. If you want to talk, let me know. Let me worry about me. You've done enough of that." Stepping into Ice's side, he wraps his arm around me and I do the same, needing and missing him. His body slowly starts to relax.

Axl shakes his head and stomps off inside and straight to the bar. "Are you going to go have a beer with your stepson?"

Ice's snarls, "All my dreams have come true. Drama, a wife, and a whiny little brat. I can die peacefully now."

Never have I heard him say something so sarcastic. The smile that lights up my face is beaming. A step or day at a time, I am in no hurry. Our love is unconventional. Will he ever give me a ring? I don't know. That's what makes it an adventure. We'll do what we want, when we are ready.

Ice

I waited until Harley was asleep in our bed. After the amount of drinks she had, she won't be up for a good eight hours. With finesse, I ease my way around the club and the brothers still in the bar area. I find my target and sit down next to Axl, with Blade on his right.

"I'm going to lay this out to you like this. ATF was hunting your mom down. I knew about it and capitalized, keeping her at my side and chained to me. I'll make no fucking apologies for what I have done except she did ask me to call you. I refused because I am a selfish fucking bastard and I didn't want to share her with her bratty ass kid. Now, you can continue with your shit or give in, understanding we are happy together, and take your ass back to Reno before you do damage to your relationship with her. I'm done with this fight. If you bring it up again, I won't be so fuckin' sweet and accommodating next time."

Blade nods his head in agreement. "Aye, brother. I

would kill any man who touched or came between me and my Ol' Lady." He holds up his beer before taking a drink. "I'm heading home in the morning." He eyes his VP to see what he'll say.

Axl rubs his chin and thinks over his options carefully. "I sure as fuck never thought I would have a daddy again. Here I am, living my own dream to get a dick for a stepdad." Axl uses my comment from before to throw in my face.

"At least that we agree on. Don't call me dad." I wrap my knuckles on the bar and take a few steps to get back into bed.

"Night, pops. Tell mom I'll call her when I get home and check in," Axl hollers out.

"Fuck my life."

"Maddy's birthday is coming up and she needs to meet her grandpa. You are bringing her grandma for that, right?"

"Axl," I turn and shock the room, "I wouldn't miss it for the world. There is so much I can teach my new granddaughter, I am looking forward to it." His face falls and is at least smart enough to keep his mouth shut.

THIRTY-TWO

Ice

Harley has her legs and arms wrapped around me. We fly down the highway, riding behind Axl and Blade. I knew she would want to see her son before he left in the morning. I wasn't about to let the prick get away without an apology either. Bright and early, I got her up and told her we had an early ride. It took some coaxing, but we made it out to the parking lot just in time.

I stood off to the side and watched them make up. She teared up and hugged her son. The way he held his mom, I knew nothing in the world could keep them apart, not me, nothing. She gave me her loyalty and stood her ground with the hardest part of her life, confronting Axl. My woman did it for me, and together we grew stronger, more trust built between us.

It was a dream come true to have her on the back of my bike. She called to me the same way the road does, like a motherfucking siren calling me home. Her breasts are pressed into my back and it's the sexiest moment I've had with her. I shared most of what is important in the world to me with her and now my bike. She has a permanent seat that no one will touch.

At the quarter mark, I lift a hand, signaling we are turning around. Both hold a peace sign down low, signaling back a safe passage home. Slowing down, I turn us around, but we don't go to the clubhouse. I take her to the one place no one has gone except a very small handful of people. We drive for a few hours until I reach a secluded house at the base of the hills behind the clubhouse. The walls are up, and I always planned on retiring here, I just didn't know when that day would come.

Harley tosses her helmet to the side and looks up at the two-story house. It's painted gray with white trim and black accents. She walks up the wood porch and gasps when she turns around, seeing the valley laid out before her. It's even more breathtaking from my spot. She took me into her heart and loved the man that she saw inside. I'm home.

Taking her hand, I lead her around our house. The walls haven't been put up yet. "Harley." She turns and the smile on her face and in her eyes is the joy that replaced the sadness a week ago. "If loving you means that I would want to die if you left, or to shelter you from pain, then I love you, Harley, with every part that I am."

Her bottom lip trembles. "I love you too, Ice. You brought me back…" She chokes on the words that are hard for her to say. She wanted to die, join the afterlife, and was scared to see if death would hurt. I showed her it wouldn't, and she chose me. Harley let the darkness ago and joined me instead. I tug her to me and kiss her mouth with a fever, taking what belongs to me, her light, her sweetness.

ICE

We don't always have to tell the whole story to know how we feel.

I give her one last peck and we finish talking about our future here together. First thing is bringing most of her stuff up here. I send a text to River to get the prospects on the road now and getting her moved up here. Harley rattles on about what kitchen she wants to have. I'll let her have it all. I couldn't care in the least. I just want her with me, that's it. Done.

We walk around the backyard and I show her the garage I have set up out back. "It has a loft built inside where we can stay until I can finish the inside of the house."

She stops and watches me closely. "You built this house?" Harley barely whispers out her question.

I raise my eyebrows. "Yes, Harley, I know how to build houses. One of my businesses is a construction company, doll. Go look at the room. I had them put your stuff inside already from the clubhouse."

Harley darts around me to go look at the small apartment loft built above the garage. She hollers, "You call this a loft? It's a very nice apartment, Ice." She shakes her head and comes down the steps and flings her arms around me.

"Good. We aren't staying in the clubhouse anymore." Tugging her along, I take her back out front of the house and we sit on the front steps. I wrap my arm around her back and her head falls onto my shoulder. Kissing the top of her head, I take a full breath of her. I breathe it all in.

Today, I want to tell her a story. "It all started with this devastatingly beautiful creature. She lured me in. Haunted my dreams with her desperation to be free of the pain. I wanted to kill her then. Strangle her with my bare hands and give her the ultimate pleasure, peace. I woke up hard countless times after dreaming of her. She would be crying with me strangling her. Not out of fear, but because she needed me to. I was her savior. For years, I was haunted by this green-eyed angel who was sad. She was my morbid fascination I never could let go of. I didn't know if my dreams would ever come true, but she was always mine. The sad girl wormed her way into me even further with her body and fire for love. She penetrated the cold barrier around my heart."

Harley's eyes are clenched tight as a tear leaks and runs down my arm. I hold onto her, never can I let her go. Every second, my bond grows stronger with her.

Her hand squeezes my arm and she rasps, "I always wondered. But somehow knew parts of it." Bringing her head up, she kisses the corner of my mouth. "Fire and ice."

"I brought you something else, hidden in my cut the whole day." From my cut, I pull out the necklace. It dangles from my hand and the charm sparkles in the sun. "I bought it because of you. I couldn't keep it when it belonged to you. This charm was what made me realize I loved you. I was so pissed you left. I never felt that way in my life."

Harley lets me place the necklace around her neck. "Ice, I'm literally just so damn happy. I love you so much. I'm always coming home to you." She holds my face in her hands, placing a hard kiss to my mouth. They will never be enough, and Harley deserves more than I can ever give her. Doesn't mean I'm not going to try. She is the fire in my heart that melted the darkness away. Harley saved my future when she thinks I saved her life.

THE END

EPILOGUE

Ice

"**T**ime to ride, boys." It's Maddison's fourth birthday. I have yet to meet Axl and Dana's daughter. He thinks he can scare me away from Harley because she has a family. Axl doesn't realize the MC has been my family, I never had a reason to extend it until now. Maddison will have her hands full when she grows up with all these men who will protect her. There is nothing that will stop me from being a part of Harley and her life, mine forever and everything that comes with it.

Harley slides onto the back seat of my bike wearing her cut with my claim stitched in, 'Property of Ice'. "Thank you," she whispers into my ear. Lightly, her teeth nip at my earlobe as she settles behind me, holding me tightly to her. My dick jerks in response even though I had her coming against the wall before we left.

It's going to be a long ride, our first together across the state. It's hot as Hades out here, perfect day to ride. The parking lot roars to life with all the engines turned on. Harley and I lead the whole club out. It's a big day, I want them to meet my granddaughter. That made Harley smile brighter than the sun when I told her where we were going today. Every stop along the way reminds me of our first trip and how far we both have come since that day.

ATF has backed off since their last agent was burnt up in a car accident and their snitch died of a drug overdose. Battle Born and I came to an understanding, I'm done with supporting their club. It's come too close to home here in Elko. Besides that, I'm not leaving Harley to go on any more stakeouts to hunt those fuckers down. I have gained more in the last month that's worth more than any money we could bargain for.

The tires play miles become a smoothing rhythm against the pavement. The hours start to blur riding across the desert, and you have time to think. Her body against mine on this road of life does something to a man. It's some kind of voodoo, a curse that can never be broken, a bond of two souls. Harley feels it too. The whole ride her hands are all over my body, rubbing my back or legs, the pull is indescribable. She is my ride or die.

Riding into Blade's territory, the scenery starts to change back to the mountains in the horizons and we drop down into the city, the parade of bikes taking up several lanes. The brothers have plans to hit the casinos and downtown bars after the party. Coming here was no hardship for them. Harley points, leading us along to Axl and Dana's home.

Outside, there is already a street full of bikes. "Park next to the house," Harley hollers over the low idle of the bike. I chuckle to myself that Axl had to buy the empty lot next door just for parking. As soon as we stop, she's up and running toward the house.

ICE

"Mimi is here, momma!" A tiny little human with green eyes runs down the driveway to Harley. She is a mix of all of them, but those eyes are Harley. Taking my time, I wander over and wait for them to get their hug out of the way. Harley has her on her hip and turns to me. "Maddy, this is Ice. He's your grandpa too, but you can call him whatever you want."

"Hmm, you don't look like my other grandpa." Her inquisitive stare looks me over thoroughly, "You bring your friends to my party?"

"Yes, these are all my friends. You look very pretty in your princess dress today." She smiles at the compliment and blushes a little. Even her little nose turns a shade of pink.

"Mimi always buys me a birthday dress and tiara." Harley plants a big kiss on her cheek, "Always birthday princess, they are special days." She wiggles out her hold and grabs Axl's hand as he approaches.

"If it isn't my favorite dad. Glad you could make it, old man." Axl hits my shoulder.

Maddy tugs at his hand while whispering loudly, "You don't have a dad, daddy."

"I know, princess."

"Then why did you say that?"

"I was being funny."

"If you say so. Come on, Poppie, bring your friends and come look to the back yard!" She takes my hand and drops her father's. He guffaws over the betrayal his daughter picked to spend time with me. "Did you and your friends bring me presents?" I can't help but laugh. Her face is tilted slightly, and she watches me waiting for the

167

answer. She is a little shark in princess clothing. I fucking love it. I would buy her a damn store to keep it there.

"I made sure of it, Maddy."

"Good." She nods. "Okay, we can have drinks now while we wait for the rest of my presents, I mean guests, to come."

"Maddy," Dana scolds. "I will cancel the party if I hear those words one more time."

"Sorry, momma." Maddy pouts. Dana releases an exhale and hugs Harley. At the same time, Maddy snickers and covers her mouth. "She won't cancel my party, now she is funny."

"Your secret is safe with me."

"I think so too." She winks then abruptly runs off when Blade arrives with his family. I love this kid. While she has the world wrapped around her finger, she makes the rules. Maddy makes me wonder if Harley and I had a kid if she would be as full of fire like this one. The answer is yes. Yes, she would.

"What are you smiling about?" Harley takes my hand in hers."

"Maddy. Those eyes drew me in just like you. Then she sealed the deal with her fire, just like you."

"I swear, Ice, if we were any younger..."

"I thought the same, doll." Losing her hand, I wrap her in my arms and whisper, "You branded me the first time you clenched around my cock. There was no going back."

"Are you ready for this?" Jazz asks my Ol' Lady. From what I knew, she's done all the brands for the Ol' Ladies. I wanted to give Harley a present of sorts and asked her to do one for my woman too. There isn't a man on earth that I want to touch her skin.

Harley turns around. "Jazzy!" She's so excited to see her, she jumps out from the bar stool. Blade's Ol' Lady owns the Black Rose bar where the after-party has started. "It's been forever. I'm so happy to see you. How long are you in town for?"

"I'm staying. For good." Jazzy turns and looks off into the crowd. The guy she looks at has his eyes trained on her. Also, the reason she's staying for good.

"It's official you two are together?" Harley holds onto her shoulders, waiting for the official news bulletin. I can't help but roll my eyes. She can't handle not having the details dragged out.

"It's official, and I'll tell you all about it, but first..." Jazz looks to me to fill in the rest.

"It's time. How about that brand, make us official?" My eyebrows raise, waiting.

"It's been official Ice," She laughs, "Absolutely, I would love to be branded by you, baby."

Life couldn't get any better and even if it does dive, Harley and I will get through the hard parts together. There is no other woman, in my opinion, more loyal than her. Jazz leads us next door to the tattoo shop where she has it all set up and ready. She hands Harley the stencil I asked her draw for me, a Royal Bastards logo with 'Property of Ice' and flames in the background.

Harley whips off her top and sits in the chair with

her back to us. She removes the bra and is naked from the waist up.

"Fuck, Harley," I growl. "How did you know where I wanted it?"

"Because I want what you want, Ice. Always have and always will."

Bending over, I kiss her shoulder. "Fucking love you, woman."

Jazzy slaps on her gloves, interrupting us. "It's not the first time I've seen her tits, and she's smoking hot. But Ice, cool off, we have some work to do."

Now I know who did the other tat for her. I stand back and watch my wife take my brand for me, for life. I am a cold-hearted bastard and take what I want with no regrets.

Featured Characters
Rancid from *New Orleans* by Crimson Syn
Diesel from *Flagstaff* by M. Merin
Grim from *Tonopah* by Nikki Landis

NOTE TO THE READERS

Thank you! I hope you loved Ice and Harley's story as much as me. They are included as side characters in my series, the Battle Born MC. You can find sneak peeks of them there. I so wanted to write their story, and I never knew for sure with all my ideas, that it would ever come true. I knew what would happen with them and it makes me extremely happy that I was given this opportunity to share what was in my head and heart with you. Hopefully, I will write a Christmas epilogue or short story for them. I just can't let them go yet!

Also, I hope to continue writing in the Royal Bastards MC and River's story would be next. Chloe's mystery of where she went will be solved. Guess who she ends up with? That's right, River. The next book I publish will be the last book for the Reno Chapter, Battle Born Series. It is Spider and Jazzy's story. Add them to your TBR now for updates. As soon as I'm done, they are going straight to publish. I put off their story to write Ice's, so I owe it to my readers to get back to them.

Follow me on Facebook and join my readers group. I would be happy to have you there and keep in touch!

ARE YOU BATTLE BORN?

First, Sign up for my newsletter to get Battle Born News!

Then be BATTLE BORN & Join the Bitches Without Borders Readers Group Page.

Find excerpts nowhere else but on my website blog at www.authorscarlettblack.com

BATTLE BORN MC SERIES IS FREE ON KU!

Money is missing and stakes are running high. Under pressure to deliver answers, the Battle Born MC take over the Reno territory while their enemies lurk in the shadows seeking vengeance. The brothers learn what the older club members did before them wasn't so easy.

Settle in for a wild ride as the brothers take down the traitors while claiming the strong women who distract them. When sparks fly and desire burns hot, truths are revealed and their pasts become entwined as they all embark on a blood thirsty hunt for retribution.

Loyalty will be tested, family will be strengthened, love will be found, and alliances will be earned as blood is spilt.

Do you have what it takes? Are you Battle Born?

ROYAL BASTARDS MC SERIES SECOND RUN

E.C. Land: *Cyclone of Chaos*
Chelle C. Craze & Eli Abbot: *Ghoul*
Scarlett Black: *Ice*
Elizabeth Knox: *Rely On Me*
J.L. Leslie: *Worth the Risk*
Deja Voss: *Lean In*
Khloe Wren: *Blaze of Honor*
Misty Walker: *Birdie's Biker*
J. Lynn Lombard: *Capone's Chaos*
Ker Dukey: *Rage*
Crimson Syn: *Scarred By Pain*
M. Merin: *Declan*
Elle Boon: *Royally F**ked*
Rae B. Lake: *Death and Paradise*
K Webster: *Copper*
Glenna Maynard: *Tempting the Biker*
K.L. Ramsey: *Whiskey Tango*
Kristine Allen: *Angel*
Nikki Landis: *Devil's Ride*
KE Osborn: *Luring Light*
CM Genovese: *Pipe Dreams*
Nicole James: *Club Princess*
Shannon Youngblood: *Leather & Chrome*
Erin Trejo: *Unbreak Me*
Winter Travers: *Six Gun*
Izzy Sweet & Sean Moriarty: *Broken Ties*
Jax Hart: *Desert Rose*
Teagan Brooks: *Shiver*

Royal Bastards MC Facebook Group
www.facebook.com/groups/royalbastardsmc

Links can be found in our Website:
www.royalbastardsmc.com

ABOUT THE AUTHOR

Scarlett Black is the author of the Battle Born MC Series. Not really knowing where a story will take her is what she loves most about writing. She strives to write about strong women and the men who love them. She believes in love and the miracles that come from it. She enjoys giving her fans a happily ever after worth melting their hearts. These may be books, but they are written with her heart and soul. She is Battle Born. Are you?

www.authorscarlettblack.com

Leave me a review on Amazon here & Follow me online!

www.goodreads.com/author/show/18204550.Scarlett_Black

www.amazon.com/author/scarlettb

partners.bookbub.com/users/sign_in

www.instagram.com/scarlett.black.author

www.facebook.com/AuthorScarlettBlack

Made in the USA
Las Vegas, NV
14 April 2023

70584891R00105